DOCTOR WHO AND THE
ARK IN SPACE

Louise

Also available in the Target series:

DOCTOR WHO
AND
THE ARK IN SPACE

Based on the BBC television serial *The Ark in Space* by Robert Holmes by arrangement with the British Broadcasting Corporation.

IAN MARTER

A TARGET BOOK

published by
the Paperback Division of
W. H. ALLEN & Co. Ltd

A Target Book
Published in 1977
by the Paperback Division of W. H. Allen & Co. Ltd
A Howard & Wyndham Company
44 Hill Street, London W1X 8LB

Second impression 1979

Printed in Great Britain by
Richard Clay (The Chaucer Press) Ltd, Bungay, Suffolk

ISBN 0 426 11631 3

Contents

Prologue: The Intruder

Out among the remotest planets, in faithful orbit through the Solar System, the great Satellite revolved slowly in the glimmer of a billion distant suns, reflecting their faint light from its cold and silent surfaces. All within remained utterly quiet and still, but primed and ready: ready for the eventual moment of awakening. Deep in its innermost structure an atomic clock oscillated, waiting for the moment when it would cause a tiny electric current to flow, activating circuits which branched throughout the vast Satellite, bringing it to life once more out in the wilderness of Space.

Patiently it waited. Then suddenly, after many centuries, something stirred within it: something alien, that was not part of its intricate programming. Panels began to slide smoothly open. Faintest shadows ran over the gleaming walls. The deserted tunnels and chambers, forming the 'rim', the 'spokes' and the 'hub' of the enormous wheel, which was the Satellite, began to echo with rustles, hoarse squeaks and whistlings. Cautiously feeling its way into one of the spherical control chambers—positioned like gigantic pods along the 'spoke' sections—there crawled an intruder. It dragged its massive leathery body along on angular tentacle-legs, which bristled with

7

sharp hairs and scratched shrilly against the metallic walls. Swinging its domed head slowly from side to side, it pierced the half-light with giant, globular eyes. At the end of its long, scorpion tail there glinted a menacing claw which clattered in the creature's wake.

As soon as it entered the control chamber, the alien intruder eagerly scanned the mass of inert instruments which covered the walls, like exhibits in an abandoned museum. From the domed ceiling there descended a shining metallic sphere. For an instant the creature was reflected in its mirror-like surface; information was flashed to a central computer bank, analysed, and a command relayed back to the sphere. It glowed brilliantly for a second. The startled intruder stared defiantly upwards, and at the same instant a fierce burst of energy sent it clattering against a control console, its tentacles contracting in agony.

For a few seconds all was still. Then the creature moved. Again the sphere glowed, and with a sharp crack hurled it back across the chamber in a blazing electrical discharge. The creature cowered, uttering hoarse screams as a stream of brutal shock-waves pulsed from the sphere, blistering its body with burns. Staring at the clusters of delicate instruments, its huge eyes useless in the fierce light, the creature began to flail at the wall panels as if searching desperately for something. All at once, a section of the panelling slid open. Fighting the searing bursts of radiation from the sphere, the creature dragged itself through the opening into a second, similar chamber. Out of range of the sphere, but now blinded and almost paralysed, the intruder fumbled among the control consoles lining the chamber until it somehow located the section it sought.

With frantic, crippled movements it ripped open the instrument panel and pulled out a thick bundle of multi-coloured cables. Then, arching its segmented tail up over its head, it gripped the cables in its huge claw and severed them cleanly with a single slice. At that moment, all through the electronic nerve centres of the Satellite, certain vital systems were closed down.

With an unearthly sigh of satisfaction the creature turned away, and in complete darkness now, crawled back through the first chamber and out into the labyrinth of tunnels and chambers. Its mission was almost completed; one final task remained. Slowly and painfully, but with deadly purpose, it made its way towards the sleeping humans. The brittle, splintering sound of its movements died away as panel after panel glided shut behind it. The sphere hung inert in the darkness.

When at last the atomic clock signalled the beginning of the great Awakening, no current flowed. The circuits remained dead, the systems did not activate. The Satellite continued its eternal orbit, the Solar Energy Reservoirs absorbing and storing energy from the sun—though no longer for any purpose.

Then there came a second invasion . . .

9

1

The Second Invasion

'Clumsy, ham-fisted idiot,' cried the Doctor, striding out of the TARDIS into pitch darkness.

'I'm terribly sorry, Doctor. I was only trying to ... trying to open the door ...' stammered Harry Sullivan, just catching the door as it swung back in his face.

'Come out of there at once, and don't touch anything else,' called the Doctor, pausing for a moment in the light streaming through the door of the TARDIS and staring about him.

The Doctor was a tall, broad man with a riot of curly brown hair bubbling out from beneath a stylish felt hat. His generous face was animated with intense curiosity as his enormous eyes peered into the semi-darkness. His hands were thrust deep into the bulging pockets of a voluminous red velvet jacket, and the trailing ends of a long multi-coloured woollen scarf flapped around his legs as he moved cautiously away from the TARDIS.

Surgeon Lieutenant Harry Sullivan RN stood uncertainly in the doorway, fiddling nervously with his cravat. He was an athletic young man in his late twenties, with a straight back and a square jaw. He wore a rowing club blazer and sharply pressed slacks.

'Oh I say,' he exclaimed, 'we've gone.'

'Who's gone, Harry?' asked a bright, laughing voice behind him.

He turned to face the mischievous smile of Sarah Jane Smith, who was watching his confusion with evident delight. Sarah was a slim, level-headed journalist, about the same age as Harry, her trim figure clad in a trendy denim trouser-suit, her short dark hair tucked into a saucy woollen hat.

'Well, I mean this isn't . . . we aren't where we were when we . . .' began Harry, venturing a step or two into the gloom. A few minutes earlier, when he had entered the old, battered blue Police Telephone Box, at the Doctor's invitation to have a quick look round, it had been standing in a corner of the Laboratory at UNIT Headquarters, in broad daylight. 'I think I've gone mad,' he muttered at last.

Sarah Jane touched his arm sympathetically. 'I know what you mean,' she said. 'That's exactly how I felt after my first trip. You'll find it takes quite a bit of getting used to.'

The door of the TARDIS swung slowly shut behind them. In the pitch darkness they could hear the Doctor moving stealthily about.

'Where are we, Doctor?' called Sarah casually. A powerful torch beam snapped on and swept round.

'Do you know, Sarah, I have no idea,' replied the Doctor after a pause. Sarah knew precisely what that little pause meant She felt her way cautiously over to the Doctor's side. The roving torchlight revealed a large spherical chamber, its walls entirely covered in instruments, with several flat control consoles, like circular tables, grouped around it.

'Just a little trip to the Caucasus, or perhaps once round the Moon'—Sarah imitated the Doctor in one of his off-hand moods—'just to prove to Harry that the old Police Box really could travel in ...'

'I didn't expect him to start fiddling with the Helmic Orientators, Sarah,' interrupted the Doctor sharply. He broke off as the chamber was dimly illuminated again. Harry had opened the door of the TARDIS and was staring into it open-mouthed.

'It's bigger than a Cathedral ... on the inside ...' he gasped in amazement. The Doctor strode over and locked the door. Still in a state of shock, Harry mumbled away in the darkness, 'You know you could make a fortune out of this thing, Doctor ...' But the Doctor was already pacing about the chamber, sweeping the torch beam over the curved reflecting walls and closely examining the dense clusters of instruments.

Grotesque shadows flapped around them. Sarah shivered. It was bitterly cold, and the air suddenly seemed terribly thin. It was quite an effort to breathe. Something loomed up against her. She jumped. It was Harry.

'Sorry, Miss Smith,' he mumbled, loosening his cravat, 'but I'm a bit disorientated ...'

'Not much oxygen,' remarked the Doctor from the shadows. 'Still,' he added cheerfully, 'nothing to worry about.'

Sarah turned to Harry. 'So suffocation is nothing to worry about,' she whispered sarcastically.

'Oh, we can survive for quite a time yet,' boomed the Doctor, suddenly right beside them. He was concentrating on spinning a yoyo effortlessly up and down its string in the torchlight.

Harry decided it was time to speak up. 'Well, I've got quite a few patients to see at four o'clock,' he tried to affect a casual air, 'so if you don't mind, Doctor, I'd like to be getting ...'

'A simple gravity reading, Harry,' grinned the Doctor, putting away the yoyo. 'It would appear that we are inside some kind of artificial satellite. Now isn't that *fascinating*.'

'Doctor, it's dark, it's cold and it's getting very airless,' Sarah protested loudly. But the Doctor had left them again, and was busily examining a section of wall panelling away on the far side of the chamber. He seemed quite oblivious of their discomfort.

Suddenly they were bathed in a harsh, unwelcoming white light.

'There we are,' cried the Doctor, turning away from the control panel and surveying the scene with childlike delight, taking in every detail of their surroundings. He seized the ends of his long scarf and spun them like propellers. 'Fascinating,' he murmured, 'fascinating.' In his resonant voice, excitement, understanding and wonder were mingled as he crept respectfully round the chamber. For a moment, his companions' discomfort gave way to amazement.

'What's it all for?' gasped Harry. He shielded his eyes from the glare and peered at the coded switches, dials, lights and buttons covering the circular wall. Despite his anxiety to return to UNIT Headquarters where he was Chief Medical Officer, he yielded to an unfortunate curiosity that had already got him into trouble in the TARDIS. He tinkered with one or two micro-switches on a nearby console.

At the same moment, an invisible panel in the wall slid open directly in front of Sarah.

'Doctor,' she cried, 'look at this.' But the Doctor was deeply engrossed in examining the bright metallic sphere which was suspended from the centre of the domed ceiling.

'Of terrestrial design certainly,' he muttered, 'but I can't quite place the period.'

'Well, none of it seems to be working now,' gasped Harry, leaning weakly against the control console in an effort to ease the increasing pain in his chest.

Sarah looked round at her two heedless companions. She knew that once the Doctor became involved in something, it was quite impossible to distract him. Besides, she had a habit of striking out on her own in search of a good front-page story. She shrugged at their indifference, and suddenly oblivious of how difficult it was becoming to breathe, stepped lightly through the opening in front of her.

She found herself in a similar, slightly smaller chamber, which was dominated by a low, couch-like construction supported on a single slender pillar in the centre of the floor. She recognised the streamlined cabinets and tape-reels of computer memory banks set into the walls. The upper part of the circular wall was patterned with blank video screens and systems display panels. Sarah leaned against the couch, her head spinning and her heart pounding. Her eyes tried to focus on a section of instrument panelling that had been ripped open, spilling out a cluster of cable ends. She suddenly found herself fighting for breath. The voices of the Doctor and Harry in the other chamber gradually receded into the distance ...

'... and judging by that modified version of the Bennet Oscillator,' the Doctor was saying, 'I would estimate that all this was put together in the Thirtieth Century.'

'Oh no,' gasped Harry. 'The Thirtieth *what*?'

'You don't agree?' Sarah heard the Doctor inquire indignantly. Harry muttered something incoherently. Then the Doctor's voice boomed confidently, 'Oh yes, the late Twenty-ninth or early Thirtieth I feel sure. For example, Harry, just look at this ...'

Sarah suddenly heard the panel glide shut behind her. She whirled round. There was no trace of it; she was confronted with a wall of blank instruments. Sarah stumbled over, her heart thumping like a steam engine, and searched for the edges of the panel.

'There must be a manual control,' she panted. She gulped for air, scarcely able to fill her lungs. In sudden panic, she pounded and kicked the panelling. 'Doctor ... please ... I can't breathe ... there's no air in here.' She felt herself gripped, as if in a huge vice. Her ears were ringing and her limbs were numbed. Desperately she clawed at the wall. 'Doctor ... Harry ... please help me ... pl ...' Sarah sank to the cold floor.

Harry was leaning against a corner of the TARDIS; despite the cold he was beginning to sweat with the effort of breathing. 'Look, Doctor ... I'm a straightforward sort of chap,' he gasped, 'are you telling me that we're now in the middle of the Thirtieth Century?'

The Doctor seemed totally unaffected by the coldness and the lack of oxygen. 'Gracious me, no, Harry,' he replied. 'Well beyond that.'

'But ... where ... *Where* are we?' pleaded Harry, not sure whether he was dreaming or going insane. The Doctor was kneeling down and listening intently to the floor through an ancient brass ear trumpet.

'Difficult to say,' he murmured, sitting back on his heels and taking a large bag of jelly-babies from his pocket. 'All this is obviously quite old,' the Doctor popped a sweet into his mouth, 'several thousand years at least.' He chewed away thoughtfully.

Suddenly he leaped to his feet. 'Where's Sarah?' he demanded, advancing on Harry who stared back at him, dumbfounded.

'Perhaps she went back into the TARDIS,' said Harry.

'Impossible,' snapped the Doctor. 'I have the key.' He strode about the chamber, peering closely at the walls through a huge magnifying glass. 'I have told her time and time again about wandering off by herself,' he said grimly.

'Well ... there ... there must be a door ... somewhere,' panted Harry, his head whirling.

The Doctor stopped in his tracks and fixed him with a piercing stare.

'Not necessarily.'

Harry glanced longingly at the TARDIS; strange and incomprehensible though it was, it suddenly seemed very familiar and safe.

'You haven't *touched* anything again, have you, Harry?' the Doctor demanded accusingly.

Harry quailed. He was feeling decidedly unwell in the airless conditions. 'No I ... well, yes I ... I think I did just press something ...'

'Show me,' commanded the Doctor.

'... but absolutely nothing happened,' protested Harry. He could barely stand upright now.

'Show me exactly what you did, Harry,' coaxed the Doctor gently.

Harry tottered over to the control console and stared down at the maze of instruments. Switches, dials and buttons danced about before his eyes in the unrelenting white glare. He struggled to remember. The Doctor's voice seemed to reach him from the other end of a long long corridor full of slamming doors:

'Just try to remember, Harry.' Harry's hand wavered uncertainly; in desperation he pressed a switch.

Immediately, the panel slid open. Sarah lay just inside the smaller chamber in a crumpled heap. At once Harry recognised the bluish pallor around her lips. 'She's cyanosed,' he whispered. 'There's even less air in there. We must get her out.'

As they bent down to lift Sarah, the panel glided shut automatically, trapping them all together. The Doctor searched feverishly for the panel control circuitry. Harry, now almost completely overcome, sank down against the wall and feebly tried to prop Sarah into a sitting position.

'All my ... m ... my fault ... sorry ...' panted Harry.

The Doctor had discovered the damaged panelling and the cluster of cable ends. He set to work with magnifier and sonic screwdriver. 'No, no, Harry, I got us into this,' he muttered, deftly sorting through the broken connections.

His movements grew rapidly heavier and clumsier as the lack of oxygen finally began to take effect. 'This ... this is quite extraordinary, Harry,' he panted. 'Gyroscopic Field Governor Circuit ...' Temperature Stabiliser ... Ah ... Oxygen Valves Servo Backup Circuits ...' Several times the Doctor dropped the sonic screwdriver and the magnifying glass. Once or twice he glanced anxiously at Sarah and Harry. They were both unconscious. Sweat ran into his eyes. His two hearts laboured. His hands felt like rubber. He forced his mind to concentrate on the delicate operation of sonic-soldering the tiny, complex connections. He kept thinking of the faithful TARDIS waiting on the other side of the vacuum panel, ready to take them all to safety—or to anywhere ...

At last, after what seemed an eternity, valves opened with a precise clicking. There was a gentle hiss of oxygen all round the chamber. Soon Harry's eyes opened. He struggled into a sitting position.

'Only just in time, Harry,' whispered the Doctor hoarsely from across the chamber. 'Are you feeling better?'

'Convalescent,' replied Harry, managing a grin. 'All I need now is a couple of weeks in Blackpool.'

They laid the unconscious Sarah gently on the couch construction, and Harry tried to revive her while the Doctor set about repairing the remaining circuits.

'There's a mystery here, Harry,' he muttered, 'Something quite extraordinary; these cables have been bitten through.'

'Bitten,' echoed Harry, all but letting Sarah tumble to the floor.

'Yes,' the Doctor continued quietly, 'and whatever was responsible clearly possessed a reasoning intelligence.'

'And very large teeth,' added Harry wryly. Sarah's eyelids flickered and then opened. 'Sarah's coming round,' he said, smiling with relief.

At that moment the panel leading to the other chamber slid smoothly aside. The Doctor strode triumphantly through. 'Splendid,' he said. 'All systems go, wouldn't you say?'

Harry checked Sarah's wavering pulse. 'Now take it easy, old girl,' he said gently, as she caught at his sleeve in a momentary spasm of fear. 'You'll be right as ninepence in a few ...' The words froze on his lips as, from the other chamber, there came a deafening crack. Harry ran across to the panel opening. The Doctor was nowhere to be seen. Something bright caught his eye. Glancing upwards he saw his own distorted reflection in the polished sphere suspended from the ceiling. Before he could step forward he was seized by one ankle and dragged to the floor. As he fell, something struck his other foot with the force of a cannonball, tearing off his shoe. He lay quite still, half under one of the control consoles. The acrid smell of burnt rubber filled the chamber. For a moment he dared not open his eyes; one foot was completely numbed, and the other was still held in an iron grip. He tried to twist himself round and sit upright. His head was at once thrust roughly back to the floor.

'Keep down, Harry,' hissed the Doctor in his ear.

Sarah lay limp on the couch. She felt as if she had floated to the surface from the bottom of a deep pool. There, in the fresh air, had been Harry's welcoming smile, but all at once he had disappeared again and she was alone. She heard the fierce cracking sounds and Harry's scream of terror. She struggled to get up, but found herself forced down on to the couch by invisible hands. Everything about her began to wobble and tiny electric shocks rippled suddenly through her entire body. She tried to call out, but no sound would come. Very slowly, and very gently, she was being pulled apart ...

Outside, in the Main Control Chamber, Harry and the Doctor crouched silently in the confined space beneath the instrument console.

'What happened?' croaked Harry at last, his throat parched with fear.

'Just don't move,' whispered the Doctor. He had balanced his hat on the end of the telescopic probe he always carried, and was stealthily inching it up into the air above the edge of the console. At once came the shattering whipcrack from above them; the hat flew into the shadows beside the TARDIS and lay smouldering. The Doctor stared at it in anguish. 'I'm afraid we're trapped again, Harry,' he sighed.

'But what *is* it?' gasped Harry.

'That,' said the Doctor, casting his eyes upward, 'is an OMDSS.'

'A what?'

'An Organic Matter Detector Surveillance System,' answered the Doctor patiently.

'A sort of electronic sentry,' suggested Harry, suddenly catching sight of the shoe that had been blown off his numb foot; it lay curled up like a charred kipper. He shuddered.

'Precisely,' said the Doctor. 'I must confess I was not expecting this—my repairs next door were a little too thorough.'

At that moment Harry's mind cleared. He craned his head to look into the adjacent chamber where they had just left Sarah, but he could not see the couch construction.

'Sarah ... keep away from the door,' he called. There was no reply. 'Sarah ... can you hear me ... Sarah?' But the only sound from the other chamber was a faint humming. Harry glanced worriedly at the Doctor, but he was totally absorbed in jiggling the metal probe about in the air. Nothing happened.

'Just as I thought,' he muttered, 'the system only reacts to organic matter in motion.'

'Well that hardly helps us,' said Harry. 'We're organic.'

'Not under here we're not,' grinned the Doctor mischievously, his voice booming in the confined space. Harry watched blankly as the Doctor adjusted the sonic screwdriver and directed it at the joint between the console support-strut and the floor. The beam of ultra-high and ultra-low frequency waves soon unsealed the sonic welds ...

'... A little to the right ... forward ... steady now. One slip, Harry, and we'll be charcoal.'

On hands and knees, sheltered by the heavy console which they carried like a giant umbrella, the Doctor and Harry inched their way across to the opposite side of the chamber. The silence from the other chamber was ominous: what if Sarah had blacked out again? Or worse, what if she suddenly came stumbling through the opening, unaware of the glittering electronic 'watchdog' in the domed ceiling?

Gradually they progressed round the chamber, the console swaying precariously in their combined grip. Even when they paused for a moment's rest, they had to support the top-heavy 'parasol' by its single centre leg. Raw-kneed and breathless with effort, Harry decided that if this really was the Thirtieth Century, then it was an awfully long way to go just to play the fool.

At last, the Doctor called a halt. 'There it is, but it's well beyond reach,' he said, craning upward. Harry was beginning to resent always being several moves behind.

'*What* is?' he asked, exasperated.

'The Surveillance System Cutout, of course,' replied the Doctor, deftly fashioning his scarf into a lasso. He flung the loop up at the switches. There was the now familiar flash and crack, and the scarf fluttered down in two blazing pieces.

'Bad luck. Good try though,' whispered Harry admiringly.

'This is not a game of cricket,' snapped the Doctor.

'Sorry,' whispered Harry, chastened. 'Mind you, if I had a ball I could jolly soon reach that switch.' The Doctor silently produced a worn cricket ball from one of his many pockets. Swallowing his amazement, Harry took it. He polished it on his lapel. His moment had come at last.

The ball, with a good off-spin to it, had scarcely left his hand than it exploded into a shower of carbon fragments. 'Organic, of course,' he muttered, crestfallen.

The Doctor leaned forward, slipped off Harry's remaining shoe, and handed it to him. 'You don't need this any more, do you, Harry?' he said significantly. Harry was becoming more and more convinced that he was in the company of a madman, with no hope of rescuing Sarah or of ever getting back to reality. He opened his mouth to speak. 'No. Good,' interrupted the Doctor. 'Now listen carefully,' and he quickly outlined a simple plan ...

... A few moments later, at a prearranged signal from the Doctor, Harry flung his shoe high over the console under which they were still hiding. At the same instant, the Doctor leapt up at the switch; there was a rapid series of cracks, a smell of burning rubber, and then silence.

After a long pause, the Doctor's head appeared

slowly over the top of the control desk, followed, after another long pause, by Harry's. Cautiously they both stood up. 'That foxed you,' said the Doctor pulling a face at himself in the mirror surface of the OMDSS. He wandered over to retrieve the remains of his hat and his scarf, calling brightly, 'It's all right now, Sarah, you can come out.'

Harry picked up his two melted shoes. 'The Brigadier will never believe a word of this,' he thought.

Suddenly the Doctor's voice sounded urgently from the other chamber. 'Sarah ... Sarah, where are you ... ?'

With a shoe in each hand, Harry padded over to the opening. The Doctor was standing alone beside the couch. All around, the chamber lights were beginning to flash on the instrument panels, and a multitude of quiet humming sounds enveloped them. The chamber seemed almost to be coming alive. The Doctor turned to Harry, his face filled with anxiety.

'Sarah's not here,' he said.

2

Sarah Vanishes

Sarah tried to scream, but the only sound she heard was a distant murmuring which grew gradually louder and more distinct. It was repeating over and over again a hypnotic refrain. 'Welcome, Sister, welcome to Terra Nova ... Welcome, Sister, welcome to Terra Nova ...'

Finding herself suddenly free of the invisible hands that had seemed to tear at her body, Sarah struggled feebly to sit up. At once the mysterious voice spoke firmly but gently. 'No, Sister, do not move. Do not attempt to leave the Tranquiller. Remain in contact with the Biocryonic vibrations.' Too weak to disobey, Sarah lay back and stared listlessly about her. She was too exhausted even to be afraid.

All she could remember was a terrifying sense of suffocation, then a brief moment of relief with the Doctor and Harry bending over her, followed by the sounds of a violent struggle and Harry's cry of distress, and finally the sensation of being slowly dismembered. The couch on which she was lying seemed familiar, but she did not remember it being encased in the translucent, glass-like canopy which now confined her. As she stared at it, the surface of the curved shield appeared to be in constant motion, just like the surface of a soap bubble. The harder she stared, so the patterns changed until they began to resemble huge, eerie shadows cast by something moving about on the other side of the glass.

The soothing voice began again, scarcely audible, and for a moment Sarah imagined that she could hear the Doctor and Harry talking, and that it was their shadows playing over the canopy. She tried to call out to them, but still she could make no sound. Panic-stricken, she attempted to hammer on the glass to attract attention, but found she could not raise her arms from the couch. She was trapped.

As before, the strange voice grew more distinct. It had a slightly mechanical tone, and echoed around her as if she were inside a vast cathedral. 'Sister, the principal phase of your Biocryogenic Processing is about to commence ...' ... Cryogenic ... cryogenic ... the word reverberated in Sarah's mind. She tried to remember; what was it? Something to do with freezing ... yes, freezing ... the theory of tissue preservation for long periods of time ... from the Greek word for frost ... She fought hard to keep hold of her train of thought, but the trance-like voice went inexorably on— '... If you have any message that you wish to be conveyed to the members of your Community, you may record it at the end of this announcement. Please preface your message with your Personal and your Community Identification Codes ...'

During the pause which followed, the space around Sarah began to fill with a white vapour that chilled her body. As it grew thicker and thicker, she felt her skin tightening and growing numb. The more she gasped with the coldness, the more the freezing vapour pierced her lungs. As it filled the capsule in which she was trapped, it seemed to solidify into a gelatinous mass; Sarah lay like a fish imprisoned in ice. She felt her blood running literally cold, her veins and arteries contracted around the chilling fluid as it coursed through her. She felt her heartbeat slowing and labouring. Her body appeared to merge into the cold jelly surrounding her. Shattering ripples burst through her as the substance began to vibrate at an ever increasing frequency. Within a few minutes, Sarah had lost all sense of her physical reality. She was aware only of her failing consciousness, and of the sound of a new voice, the quiet, authoritative voice of an elderly woman.

'Greetings, Sister Volunteer. On behalf of the World Executive, I, the High Minister, salute you who are about to make the supreme sacrifice. In a moment you will pass beyond life. Lest there should remain any doubt in your mind or fear in your heart, remember; you take with you not only your own, but all our pasts. We, who remain to perish here, will live again in you. You are our only future ... our only hope ...' The voice finally faded into silence, and with it, Sarah lost consciousness. After a while, the white substance thinned and finally vapourised and disappeared. When it cleared, the couch was empty.

'Harry, I am an idiot.' The Doctor and Harry were bending anxiously over the couch on which, five minutes earlier, they had placed the semi-conscious

27

Sarah. While they had been fighting their duel with the OMDSS in the other chamber, Sarah had apparently disappeared into thin air. Having satisfied himself that there were no more concealed panels through which she could have gone, the Doctor had removed a part of the upholstered section of the couch, and exposed a honeycomb of small cells, each about the size and shape of the reflector in a bicycle lamp. The cells were inter-connected with fine coppery wiring embedded in a perspex frame.

Harry was relieved that, just for once, he was not to blame for what had happened.

'Fortunately it's only an internal relay,' said the Doctor, glancing up at one of the instrument displays set into the circular wall.

'A what?' Harry looked from the couch to the instrument panel and back to the Doctor.

'A short-range Matter Transmitter,' snapped the Doctor, striding back into the main chamber. Harry padded after him, still clutching the remains of his shoes.

'What on earth does *that* mean?'

'It means,' called the Doctor, stepping through another panel in the main chamber which opened automatically as he approached it, 'that Sarah can't be very far away. Do come along, Harry.'

Slithering on the smooth metal flooring, Harry followed. As he entered the long tunnel-like passage leading from the chamber, he was amazed to see that the Doctor had already reached the other end and was waiting impatiently for him. All at once, Harry's feet were swept from under him, and he found himself sitting on a moving track running down the centre of the tunnel. It carried him smoothly with a faint hum to the far end. Just as he scrambled to his feet, convinced that he was about to crash headlong into the bulkhead at the end of the tunnel, the track slowed and stopped. Harry had no time to express his astonishment; the Doctor was already disappearing through a panel he had opened in the bulkhead wall.

They found themselves at a 'T' junction, where the tunnel joined at right angles with a spacious gallery which curved away out of sight in both directions. The Doctor motioned Harry to stay where he was, then advanced cautiously into the middle of the intersection. All the surfaces of the gallery were made of the same highly reflective metal, and a harsh white light flooded everywhere from a concealed source. Along the outer wall of the gallery, at intervals of a few metres, were set large ovoid window panels of tinted glass, through which a brilliantly clear night sky blazed. It was clearer than Harry had ever seen it before.

'I say,' he breathed. 'It's beautiful ...' The words faded from his lips as he realised with a start that the billions of stars were moving slowly but unmistakably across the panels. He felt momentarily unsteady, as if a ship's deck were heaving beneath his feet. 'We're ... we're *moving*,' he said, his eyes wide.

'This is no time for star-gazing, Harry,' called the Doctor, setting off briskly to the left. When Harry finally tore his eyes away from the splendid panorama through the observation panels, the Doctor had already disappeared round the curve.

'This must be the size of a running track,' panted Harry, as he hurried to catch up.

'Naturally.' The Doctor grinned over his shoulder. 'We are now in the Cincture Structure.'

'The what?' Harry skidded in his stockinged feet.

'The outer wheel,' called the Doctor. 'We appear to be inside an old Centrifugal Gravity Satellite, shaped rather like a doughnut with an éclair stuck through the middle and connected to it by several chocolate fingers.'

Harry rather resented the Doctor's oversimplified explanation. 'I suppose we are now walking round inside a doughnut,' he remarked. But his sarcasm was lost on the Doctor.

'Exactly,' he said. 'Of course it has been converted to a more sophisticated Electrostatic Field Gravity System, but it still revolves on its axis because there's simply nothing to stop it.'

They were approaching another bulkhead. In the centre of its sealed panel there was a stencilled notice in green and maroon striped computer lettering:

FIRST TECHNOP MEDTECH PERSONNEL ONLY

Just before they reached it, the Doctor darted suddenly through yet another automatic panel which opened silently in the inner side wall. He re-emerged immediately, much to Harry's relief. 'Well, Sarah's not in *there*,' he said, striding on towards the bulkhead barring their way. All at once a disembodied metallic voice barked at them: 'STERILE AREA'.

The Doctor paused in his tracks, and Harry leaped backwards as if he had trodden on a nail. All these hidden, automatic panels, electronic guards, hidden voices and moving floors made him feel as if he were trapped in a crazy maze at a funfair. However the Doctor seemed perfectly at home; he had rested his head against a small copper plate at the side of the bulkhead panel, and seemed to be meditating. After a few seconds the panel opened.

'How did you do that?' exclaimed Harry.

'Alpha waves and things,' the Doctor tapped his head. 'It's surprising what one can do with a little thought.' He ushered Harry through the opening.

'Do you think we should?' asked Harry anxiously, remembering the curt, nightmarish announcement they had just heard.

'Probably not,' grinned the Doctor mischievously, turning to close the panel behind them.

At that moment, Harry caught a glimpse of something moving, just at the point where the gallery ahead curved out of sight. Something appeared to slither quickly across the floor; he had a momentary impression of a pulsating cluster of fluorescent bubbles, and of a faint crackling sound like toffee paper. He froze, speechless with fright, then grabbed the Doctor's sleeve.

'Doctor, there's something there,' he whispered, pointing to the spot. The gallery stretched in a graceful arc, the bright stars gliding slowly across the observation panels.

The Doctor looked doubtful. 'Trick of the light, Harry,' he shrugged.

'No. I saw something moving,' Harry insisted. He crept forward a few metres. Suddenly he found his stockinged feet glued firmly to the floor. He gave a startled yelp, and looked slowly down. He had stepped on a faint, silvery trail of sticky substance—about thirty centimetres wide—which traversed the gallery from wall to wall.

The Doctor knelt down and examined it closely through his magnifier. 'Fascinating,' he exclaimed at last. 'Just like the track left by a gastropod mollusc.'

Harry stared incredulously at him. 'A snail? *That* size?' He tore his feet free from the adhesive trail, leaving wisps of wool stuck fast to the floor. 'That's impossible, Doctor, and anyway, how could it have got through there?' Harry pointed to the fine-mesh grille set into the base of the inner wall, into which the trail disappeared. The Doctor grunted, tracing the silver track across the gallery and up the outer wall where it disappeared into a similar grille set between two of the window panels.

'A multi-nucleate organism perhaps?' he said.

Harry's confidence began to return. Here was a subject about which he felt he knew something. 'But surely, Doctor, such an organism would not be capable of moving that fast ...'

'Come on,' interrupted the Doctor, 'let's find Sarah first. Ah, this looks promising.' He strode towards a panel in the inner wall, a few metres along from the grating. As before, he knelt down and rested his forehead against the small plate set into the wall, frowning in profound concentration. Nothing happened; the panel remained shut. The Doctor stood up for a moment and mopped his brow, then he leaned forward and tried again, his face creased with effort. After a long pause, Harry jumped as the panel suddenly zipped open. Even the Doctor looked a trifle surprised.

'That must have been *some idea* you had.' Harry grinned admiringly.

The Doctor shrugged. 'Oh, just a little notion for a new opening gambit in four-dimensional chess.'

They stepped into a small cubicle resembling a lift. The panel closed behind them. They stood awkwardly nose to nose.

'Well, she's obviously not in here . . .' began Harry wearily. A rapid series of extremely uncomfortable sensations pulsed through his entire body, as if it were expanding to the size of an elephant and at once contracting to that of a flea, and then expanding again in quick succession.

'Decontamination Chamber,' said the Doctor, quite unaffected. Harry felt as if he were being shaken to a jelly. 'Ultra high and low frequency oscillations,' the Doctor added casually, 'confuses the microbes—much more efficient than your old-fashioned antibiotics.'

When the vibrations stopped, a second panel opened in the opposite wall, revealing a long straight tunnel bathed in soft greenish light. Another moving track carried them smoothly and swiftly along it.

'This must lead to the central hub-structure,' said the Doctor eagerly. He continued to mutter to himself, gesturing from side to side at the fluorescent systems-displays which lit up one by one as they

33

passed. Harry struggled to keep upright as they glided along, his head whirling like a stone at the end of a long string. Without warning, the Doctor put out his hand towards the wall of the tunnel and the conveyor stopped moving. Harry all but fell flat on his face.

The Doctor was staring at a large, complex display marked:

NEURO ADVANCE/RETARD PULSORS

The display consisted of a mass of regularly arranged, tiny neon lamps with illuminated connecting circuits. Some were pulsing weakly, others were inactive, and a few were flashing strongly with a long slow rhythm. The Doctor's eyes widened: 'Harry, do you realise what all this is?' he said excitedly, removing his hand from the wall and setting the floor in motion again with a jerk. 'It's a complete Cryogenic Suspension System inside a converted Navigation Satellite.' But Harry scarcely heard; he was still clutching his aching head. The Doctor stopped the conveyor every few metres to examine the complex displays of coded circuitry which lit up as if by magic. He grew more and more animated. 'There's not the slightest doubt ...' he cried ... 'Fascinating ...' Harry could only manage a groan of pain and confusion.

When they reached the far end of the softly-lit tunnel, they were confronted with yet another panel. It bore a stencilled identification:

ACCESS CHAMBER: FIRST TECHNOP MEDTECH PERSONNEL ONLY

The Doctor immediately took out his ear trumpet and placed the horn against the bulkhead frame. He listened intently for a while. 'We're in luck, Harry,' he said at last. 'The release-lag relay has operated—we can go in.' Harry was not at all sure that was a good thing, but he was in no condition to protest.

They entered a 'fat' crescent-shaped chamber, much larger than those they had already seen. One entire half of the straighter wall was patterned with a multi-coloured chequer-board of tiny coded panels. On the other side of a large access panel in the centre of the wall, there was a series of semi-circular observation ports emitting a faint, bluish light. Opposite, set into the inner wall of the crescent, was a couch, identical to the one in the Control Chamber from which Sarah had disappeared, except that this one was covered by a curved transparent shield. Control consoles, elegant flat structures supported on single struts, were grouped all round the chamber. The subdued lighting gave the chamber a solemn, church-like atmosphere.

'We're getting warm, Harry,' said the Doctor, striding over to examine first the couch, then the control consoles.

Harry shivered; on the contrary, it seemed to him to be decidedly chillier in here. He tottered over and leaned against the chequered section of wall, still feeling the effects of the Decontamination Chamber. He stared across at the empty couch. 'Well, she certainly isn't *here*,' he said.

Totally absorbed, the Doctor darted over to peer through the observation ports: *'Balaenoptera mus-*

culus,' he exclaimed, his eyes brightening.

'The Blue Whale,' Harry translated mechanically. Then he froze.

Something had touched him on the shoulder from behind, and pushed him firmly away from the wall. He staggered forward, mute with terror, and collapsed in a heap. The Doctor glanced round. His enormous eyes opened wide. He leaped over the spreadeagled Harry with a cry. Harry dared not turn his head.

'Just look at *this*,' the Doctor shouted delightedly. One of the little coded panels had sprung open, revealing itself to be a long narrow drawer, packed with what looked like miniature tape cassettes. The Doctor quickly opened several others. 'Everything they considered worth preserving,' said the Doctor slowly. 'Architecture ... Electronics ... Agriculture ... Music ... the sum of human knowledge ... here.'

'Who ... I mean what for ... ?' muttered Harry, hauling himself to his feet.

'Posterity?' shrugged the Doctor, wandering thoughtfully round the chamber. He suddenly stopped directly in front of Harry. 'What's missing, Harry?' he demanded. Harry was about to point out that for one thing Sarah was missing, when the Doctor seized him by the arm and marched him over to the observation ports. Harry screwed up his eyes and peered into one marked ANIMAL AND BOTANIC.

Dim shapes hung in the cobalt gloom. For a moment Harry thought he glimpsed an elephant—or rather two elephants—and something that looked very like a palm tree. He backed away, rubbing his

36

eyes. 'Please, Doctor,' he implored, 'the straight-forward human mind isn't capable of ...'

'Exactly,' the Doctor smiled. 'Man—The Human Species is quite conspicuously absent.' He sat down and gestured around him. 'If we assume that some catastrophe occurred on Earth and that, before the end, this Satellite was converted to function as a Cryo-genic Preservation System ...'

'A sort of Noah's Ark,' said Harry. The Doctor nodded ...

'... The missing element is Man himself. What has happened to the Human Species, Harry?' The Doctor fixed Harry with a penetrating stare and leaned back on the instrument panel, his elbow de-pressing a series of touch-buttons ...

From behind the reflecting surfaces of the chamber walls came the subdued clatter of relays operating. With a sonorous humming, a section of the wall slid slowly aside. The space beyond was filled with a faint, iridescent glow quite unlike anything Harry had ever seen. A wave of coldness enveloped them, as if a long imprisoned breath had been released from the phosphorescent depths with an almost audible sigh. It was as if the chamber beyond were whispering to itself.

Awestruck, Harry followed the Doctor over to the opening, and stood at his shoulder. They were on the threshold of an immensely tall chamber composed of three semicircular bays arranged around a broad shaft rising through the centre. At its widest, the chamber was at least thirty metres across. Alcoved sections, each containing a covered pallet, were grouped side by side around the bays. The rows of recessed pallets were ranged in storeys stretching out of sight into pitch darkness above them, and each storey was surrounded by a narrow gallery connected to the circular central shaft by catwalks. The criss-cross of glinting metal tracery reminded Harry of the framework of an airship stood on end.

The phosphorescent light filling the chamber came from the translucent shields protecting the pallets; each shield was moulded to the contours of the human form. As their eyes became accustomed to the alien half-light, the Doctor and Harry discerned the outline of a human body suspended in each alcove. In the cold silence the effect was like that of entering a huge mausoleum.

'What a pl ...' began Harry. His voice rang and reverberated round the chamber. He went on in an abashed whisper, 'What a place for a Mortuary. Look, Doctor, there must be *hundreds* of them.'

The Doctor advanced a few paces, craning upwards with an air of respect. 'This is no Mortuary, Harry. Quite the reverse. It's an old principle, but I've never seen it applied on this scale before.'

As they began to walk slowly round, staring up at the seemingly endless array of bodies, Harry tried to conceal his unease beneath an air of professional detachment. 'When you've seen one corpse you've seen them all,' he shrugged.

The Doctor wandered into the shadows of the next bay, peering through the shields as if examining exhibits in a museum. 'These people are not dead, Harry, they're asleep.' He continued to speak, his voice rising and echoing majestically around the vast vaults. '... Homo Sapiens ... what an indomitable species ... it is only a few million years since it crawled up out of the sea and learned to walk ... a puny defenceless biped ... it has survived flood, plague, famine, war ... and now here it is out among the stars ... awaiting a new life. That's something for you to be proud of, Harry ... *Harry*! What do you think you are doing?'

The Doctor had made a complete circuit of the chamber, and come upon Harry examining the pupils of an occupant whose shield he had managed to prise open. Harry pointed to the slim, fair-haired young man lying there inert with open, staring eyes. He was dressed in a simple white uniform with green identification flashes. There was no colour in his face, and his skin was waxen and cold.

'There you are, Doctor,' said Harry triumphantly, 'not a flicker of life.'

'Suspended Animation,' retorted the Doctor, pushing Harry aside and quickly closing the shield.

'But there are no metabolic functions at all,' protested Harry. 'Even in the deepest coma you will find that the ...'

'Total Cryogenic Suspension, Harry,' the Doctor interrupted impatiently. 'You can't survive ten thousand years in a coma.'

Harry stared at the shrouded figure. 'Ten ... thousand years?' he said. 'That's impossible ...'

'Oh, ten thousand ... fifty thousand—the time is immaterial. Provided, of course, that no one interferes with the systems,' the Doctor added pointedly. Harry glanced wildly about at the ranks of inert human bodies, his mind reeling. The Doctor spoke in an almost reverent hush. 'The future of the entire human race in one chamber.'

Carefully he checked that the pallet Harry had opened was firmly closed and sealed again. 'Come along, Harry,' he said. 'We must find Sarah, and then take our leave. We're intruders here.'

Anxious not to irritate the Doctor any further, Harry resisted the flood of questions rising in his mind and followed him towards the entrance. As he turned for a last look at the awesome spectacle, Harry's heart missed a beat; his shoeless feet were suddenly held in a fierce grip that all but toppled him over.

'Doctor, look,' he breathed. He was stuck fast to another silvery trail snaking across the floor of the chamber. It was identical to the one they had found earlier. It disappeared into a grille at the base of the central shaft.

The Doctor dropped to his knees and began tracing the sticky trail as it wound away into the shadows.

'Perhaps it's some kind of mould,' suggested Harry.

'But you said you saw something moving before,' the Doctor reminded him. Harry shivered and looked uneasily around. He remembered the Doctor's reference to giant snails.

Something caught his eye in one of the pallets in the opposite bay. It looked different from the others. The Doctor was busy trying to scrape off a sliver of the tacky substance with the probe. On tip-toe, his socks still sticking slightly to the floor, Harry cautiously approached the pallet. As he peered into it, he thought he detected a swirling, vaporous movement. Glancing round to make sure the Doctor was still occupied, Harry eased open the magnetic shield ...

There, her skin like chalk and her body cold and rigid, lay Sarah Jane Smith. For a moment Harry was speechless, riveted by Sarah's fixed, expressionless gaze. Then he gasped 'Sarah ...'

The Doctor was at his side in an instant, ready to reprove him for his meddlesome ways. When he saw Sarah his huge eyes nearly popped out of his head. Very quietly he said, 'There's nothing we can do for her, Harry.' Instinctively Harry moved forward to lift Sarah out of the pallet. The Doctor firmly gripped him by the arm. 'We're too late,' he whispered. 'She's become part of the process. We'll only harm her if we interfere now.'

Harry stared at him in horror. 'There must be something I can do,' he cried.

Shaking his head firmly, the Doctor started to close the magnetic shroud. 'Sarah will remain like that for a thousand years at least.'

'Not if I can help it,' said Harry defiantly. Earlier he had noticed the outlines of coded inspection panels set into the central shaft. He gestured hopefully towards them. 'Couldn't we break into the works?' he pleaded. 'Reverse the process or something?' But again the Doctor shook his head resolutely.

On a sudden impulse, Harry darted across to the shaft and began clawing frantically at the smooth, sealed edges of the panels. Before the Doctor could restrain him, he had sprung open a hatch the size of a door. He found himself staring into a dark cubicle, and for a split second he caught a glimpse of an enormous locust-like figure with gigantic eyes, looming over him like an insect Buddha. Then, as he sprang backwards with a scream of terror, something toppled slowly past him with a sickening crunching sound. There was a clatter of brittle tentacles and antennae which fractured and scattered a gelatinous cobweb substance all over him.

3

Sabotage!

Harry stood with his back pressed against the curved wall of the shaft. He was trembling, and his face was beaded with sweat. He stared at the enormous 'insect' which lay crumbling at his feet. The surface of its segmented body was a glossy indigo colour; here and there were patches of twisted and blackened tissue, like scorched plastic. The six tentacular legs bristled with razor-sharp 'hairs'. The creature's octopus head contained a huge globular eye on each side, and each eye was composed of thousands of cells in which Harry saw himself reflected over and over again. The creature was fully three metres long from the top of its domed head to the tip of the fearsome pincer in which its tail terminated.

At last Harry managed to speak. 'At least it's dead,' he gasped.

The Doctor calmly picked up a shattered length of tentacle which powdered and crumbled in his fingers. 'Practically mummified,' he nodded.

'Just look at the size of its brain pan,' said Harry, his fear gradually giving way to fascination.

'Clearly a creature of considerable intelligence,' murmured the Doctor, taking out his magnifying glass and probe. He knelt down beside the massive corpse.

'But what *is* it?' Harry asked, amazed at the Doctor's apparently fearless curiosity. The Doctor always liked to have a ready answer for his insatiably inquisitive human companions, but this was one occasion when he found himself rather at a loss. He did not answer, but became totally absorbed in an anatomical investigation.

Harry remained with his back firmly against the shaft, afraid to move. He looked across at Sarah. She seemed to stare straight back at him, her face an impassive mask. Harry imagined the open eyes of all the other humans 'sleeping' in the vast chamber, staring sightlessly at their own reflections in the polished surfaces, for perhaps thousands of years the Doctor had said, their bodies without heartbeat or consciousness, yet alive.

Suddenly he felt a prickling sensation at the back of his neck. In one of the pallets the phosphorescent glow seemed to have intensified. It grew rapidly brighter until he could hardly bear to look at it, and the silhouette of the occupant appeared to undulate with the same rhythm as an eerie wobbling hum that filled the chamber and made Harry cover his ears. The glare and the vibrations overwhelmed him for a moment. When he came to, he saw the Doctor standing motionless in front of the pallet which was now quiet again. The shield was open. Harry moved cautiously round the central shaft to avoid the huge crumbling corpse, and padded across the chamber to join the Doctor.

The pallet was occupied by a dark-haired woman in her thirties, wearing the same simple white uni-

44

form with green flashes as the young man Harry had examined earlier. But the young woman's skin was glowing with healthy colour, and Harry noticed that her pupils were dilating and contracting. She lay with her arms at their sides, palms outward. In her wrist, Harry's practised eye caught the beat of a regular pulse.

Suddenly, her slim body arched in a spasm of pain; then it relaxed with a gasping intake of breath. She lay panting for a few moments, her head rolling from side to side. Then her eyes focussed on the Doctor. A shadow of incomprehension passed across her face. Slowly she brought her hands together and stared at them. Then she looked up again at the Doctor, her fingers making urgent grasping movements.

'Please do not be alarmed,' the Doctor said gently. 'We are friends.'

'She wants us to help her up,' said Harry, hurrying forward.

'No, Harry. I think this is what she needs.' The Doctor leaned across and took a small transparent container from a holder fitted to the inside of the pallet cover. Visible inside the container were several coloured spheres, like billiard balls, and a gleaming instrument resembling a spray gun.

'I shouldn't have opened the shield,' muttered the Doctor, watching intently as the woman eagerly took out the spray gun, and carefully fitted one of the small spherical objects into the base of the handle. She then pressed the star-shaped nozzle against her forehead and operated a button. There was a brief high-pitched whirr. The woman's body convulsed, and then went limp. After a few moments, she rose gracefully from the pallet and stood motionless, fixing the Doctor and Harry with a piercing stare. She was fully two metres tall, and even the Doctor seemed a little disconcerted by her detached, authoritative air. She betrayed no emotion at her awakening.

'Explain your presence here,' she suddenly ordered in a toneless, clinical voice. She seemed neither surprised nor afraid.

'Well, there's very little to explain,' began the Doctor amiably. 'We are travellers in space and time like yourself.'

The woman walked slowly round them. 'That is not adequate,' she retorted.

Harry felt extremely uncomfortable under her cold, relentless stare. 'My name's Sullivan ... Surgeon Lieutenant Harry Sullivan ... and this ... this is the Doctor,' he mumbled.

The woman's eyes widened. 'You claim to be Medtechs?' The note of incredulity in her voice suddenly made her seem a little more human.

'Oh, my Doctorate is purely honorary,' said the Doctor with a conciliatory smile, 'and Harry here is ...'

The woman raised her hand imperiously for silence. 'My name is Vira. I am First Medtech,' she announced.

'How very fortunate,' said the Doctor. 'We have a dear young friend over there who needs your help desperately.' He pointed across the chamber to where Sarah lay.

For a moment, Vira stared at the Doctor, evidently

46

on her guard. Then she walked gracefully across to Sarah's pallet. She looked at Sarah without emotion. 'The female is an intruder, like yourselves,' she said icily. Vira turned abruptly away, as if losing all interest in them. 'She was not among the Chosen,' she said, looking round at the inert and shadowy forms surrounding them. She appeared to be listening, waiting—her eyes alert and shining.

'Well, she's among the Chosen *now*, isn't she?' blurted out Harry. Vira turned a withering, blank stare upon him. Harry retreated a step and bit his lip, regretting his sarcasm.

The Doctor intervened gently. 'Is there any method of reversing the Cryogenic function at this stage?'

'It would be dangerous,' Vira replied distantly. 'Is the female of value?'

This was too much for Harry. 'What kind of question is that?' he exploded, wincing as the Doctor stood firmly on his stockinged toes.

'She is of great value to us,' the Doctor said quietly.

Vira hesitated a moment, then passed her hand over a section of the pallet frame, activating a small fluorescent systems display. 'Neural activity is rapidly receding,' she declared. 'I will discharge a monod block.' Vira took out the instruments from the pallet kit, and repeated the procedure she had performed upon herself earlier. She pressed the probe against Sarah's temple and triggered the charge. 'The female will revive soon, or die,' she said flatly, replacing the equipment in the holder. 'At this stage, the action of anti-protonic is not predictable.'

Vira turned. On the far side of the chamber, the

47

pallet next to her own was beginning to glow and to emit the same pulsing hum which had heralded her own awakening. There was a sudden yielding in her face. 'Commander,' she whispered, crossing swiftly into the vibrating glare. 'This is our Prime Unit—Noah.'

Harry shielded his eyes, and turned to the Doctor.

'As in Noah's Ark, eh?' he said.

'Your colony speech has no meaning,' said Vira. 'We called him Noah as an amusement.'

'A joke,' Harry corrected her.

Vira nodded gravely, her eyes fixed on the incandescent shield of the pallet. 'There was not much joke in the last days,' she added quietly.

The Doctor moved to her side. Like Vira, he seemed unaffected by the fierce light. 'What happened during those last days on Earth?' he asked gently.

Without taking her eyes from the pallet, Vira replied in amazement, 'Has your colony no records? Where are you from?'

'Well, Harry's from Earth, and I ...' began the Doctor.

'That is not possible,' said Vira. 'The solar flares destroyed all life on the Earth.'

The Doctor nodded. 'Of course, solar flares.'

Vira opened the shield, now that the radiation had subsided, and checked the pallet systems-display. 'We calculated that it would be ten thousand years before the biosphere became viable again,' she said.

'At the very least,' agreed the Doctor. 'But I think

48

you have overslept by several thousand years. When we arrived, we found a massive systems failure. Your alarm clock failed to work.'

Vira shook her head. 'The systems have a negative fault capacity,' she replied sharply.

The Doctor took her firmly by the arm. 'Possibly,' he said. 'But at some time you have had other visitors besides ourselves.' He led Vira across the chamber into the bay beyond the central shaft, where the monstrous corpse of the locust-like creature lay in the shadows. Vira showed no fear, only surprise. The Doctor watched her reaction closely. 'A truant from your Animal and Botanic Section perhaps?' he suggested.

'What is it?' Vira demanded suspiciously.

'I don't know yet,' said the Doctor, peering into one of the creature's great yellow eyes. 'But it had some purpose in coming here ...'

'What purpose?' said Vira, suddenly tense, her eyes roaming over the ranks of softly glowing pallets stretched all around and above them.

Before the Doctor could reply, she turned with a gasp and sped across the chamber to Noah's pallet. The quiet, rhythmic pulse of light and sound had become irregular and staccato. 'There is a fault in the Bionosphere,' she cried in disbelief. She wrung her hands in desperation. Harry was amazed at her sudden helplessness.

The Doctor swiftly ran his eye over the systems-display. 'There is an optimum overload in the central power supply,' he said. 'We must prevent a cascade tripout.'

Vira gestured to the other pallets in the bay. 'But we have no Technops, Doctor,' she cried. 'The Programme was planned so that First Technops and First Medtechs would undergo simultaneous Revivification.' Again she stared suspiciously at them. 'There has been interference,' she added threateningly.

The Doctor strode towards the Access Chamber. 'I think I can help you,' he said. 'Harry, you keep an eye on Sarah while I'm gone.' Before Vira could protest he ran out of the chamber.

Meanwhile, deep in the Infrastructure of the Satellite, far down inside the central hub of the great wheel where, little by little over the centuries, energy from the pale and distant Sun had been focussed and stored in huge reservoirs, a voracious alien life-form had established its lair. The surfaces of many of the spherical reservoirs were covered in a glistening, bubbling substance which pulsated in the dull amber glow of the chamber. Here and there, along the conduits connecting one reservoir to another, slid clusters of viscous matter which stretched out and then gathered again into globules with a dry crackling sound.

As it spread slowly over the surface of the reservoirs, the substance became denser, more opaque and brittle. Occasionally the crackling globules formed weird, nightmare shapes which swelled and then burst into long, twisting fronds, hissing and spitting like snakes. Colossal quantities of the precious energy were absorbed by the parasite bubbles, so that the vital systems of the Satellite were increasingly starved of essential power . .

The Doctor swiftly made his way from the Cryogenic Section back to the Control Centre where the TARDIS had materialised. As he hurried along the softly-lit tunnels, he paused briefly to examine fresh trails of the tacky, silver substance clinging to the floors, walls and even ceilings. He was rapidly becoming convinced that something was, at that very moment, engaged in a destructive attack on the Satellite from within. He crept with the stealth of a predator stalking its prey—well aware that he himself might be the prey of an as yet unknown enemy. Reaching the smaller Control Chamber, from which Sarah had disappeared, the Doctor set to work with the sonic screwdriver, skilfully rearranging a mass of circuits in an attempt to provide sufficient power to the Cryogenic systems.

As he worked, he was aware of an insidious, evil force infiltrating the innermost parts of the Satellite; a hidden enemy ready to attack at any moment.

In the Cryogenic Chamber, Harry waited helplessly at Sarah's side while Vira concentrated on the life and death struggle of her own people. She glided from pallet to pallet, checking the systems-displays, and occasionally administering treatment with an array of instruments whose function Harry could only guess at.

'I should have gone myself,' she said at last, returning to Noah's pallet. 'You are Dawn Timers; your companion has no knowledge of our Satellite.'

'Oh, he's an absolute wizard with bits of wire and things,' said Harry with desperate optimism. 'He'll have it all ticking over in no time.'

At that moment the oscillations in Noah's pallet settled into a steady rhythm again. Vira checked the display, then she turned to Harry. 'The fault has corrected,' she smiled. 'Noah will soon revive.'

'Harry?' The Doctor's voice boomed out in the adjacent Access Chamber. Harry hurried through. Over the intercom the Doctor asked whether the power had been restored in the Cryogenic systems. He said that his lash-up in the Control Centre would not be adequate for very long, and that he suspected a major fault in the Solar Stacks. 'I'm going down to take a look, Harry,' he boomed.

'O.K., Doctor,' said Harry apprehensively. 'But don't be too long ...' There came an uncommunicative grunt from the intercom and then silence. Harry padded back into the Cryogenic Chamber, to find Vira stretching out her hand in greeting to a tall, slim but powerful man with short black hair and a trim beard. He was holding out his hands to her in a simple gesture of recognition.

'Then it is ended, Vira. We are alive again,' the man said gently.

'And together, Commander,' smiled Vira.

Feeling rather superfluous, Harry wandered across to Sarah's pallet, and stood watching for a flicker of returning consciousness.

'Who is this?' Harry swung round at the ice-cold enquiry. Noah was staring at him with blazing eyes.

'The name's Sullivan ... sir,' Harry began.

Noah turned to Vira in disbelief. 'A regressive ... here?' he exclaimed.

'I'm no regressive,' retorted Harry, 'I am a Naval Officer.'

'Clearly a Regressive—the speech patterns are unmistakable,' said the Commander in a hollow, detached tone that sent a shiver through Harry. Vira explained briefly about the Doctor and his companions. Noah continued to stare at Harry with intense hostility. 'There was a Regressive element among the volunteers for Colony Seven,' he said at last. He looked Harry up and down, staring at his crumpled clothes and shoeless feet in undisguised disgust. 'Our Genetic Pool has been refined to the ultimate,' Noah almost shouted, turning upon Vira. 'You must be aware that three random units could threaten our survival ... and the contamination factor ... irrevocable damage may already have occurred.'

Suddenly there came a gasp from behind Harry. He whirled about, and was delighted to see that Sarah's eyelids were flickering. He took her hands. 'Come on, old girl,' he cried. 'I know you can do it.'

Vira hesitated a moment under her Commander's furious gaze. Then she said quietly, 'The Council can decide, Commander,' and walked quickly over to Sarah's pallet, and began monitoring her progress. 'Your companion had not reached total metabolic suspension,' she murmured to Harry. 'She will revive soon.'

Harry took a step towards the Access Chamber. 'We must tell the Doctor.'

Noah approached Harry menacingly. 'Where is the third Regressive?' he demanded.

'He's having a look at your ... er ... Solar Stacks,' said Harry in euphoric relief at Sarah's imminent recovery. 'He reckons they're on the blink.'

'The Solar Reservoirs,' hissed Noah. 'He must be stopped.' The Commander spun round and ran from the chamber.

His improvised rearrangement of the main power circuits completed, the Doctor quickly found his way from the Control Centre down into the very heart of the Satellite. As he opened shutter after shutter, on his guard for whatever might be lurking on the other side, he puzzled over Harry's description of the bubbling phenomenon he had seen, and tried to relate it to the gigantic corpse they had discovered in the Cryogenic Chamber. He encountered more and more silver trails criss-crossing the tunnels, emerging from and disappearing into the grilled openings.

He soon found himself confronting a large circular door, similar to that of a strongroom, bearing a stark warning in luminous stencilling:

SOLAR PLASMA CELLS

EXTREME RADIATION HAZARD

FIRST TECHNOPS ONLY

The Doctor smiled to himself; after a few minutes' juggling with ear trumpet, pocket magnet and probe, he succeeded in operating the lock. The door—a fifty centimetres thick Radiation Shield—swung open smoothly. Cautiously the Doctor entered the vast hemispherical chamber. His eyes adapted immediately to the subdued orange glow within. One by one he began examining the ceramic plasma bottles— translucent spheres five metres in diameter.

'Well, well,' he murmured, 'the old vacuum plasma method—with a few little refinements. They must have been in a hurry to leave Earth. Not a bad lash-up at all.'

Everything seemed to be in order. Then the Doctor detected, amid the almost imperceptible humming of the chamber, a brittle crackling sound, which was growing steadily louder and closer. He crouched beneath one of the reservoirs and listened. Although there was no sensation of hotness from the super-heated plasma, the Doctor knew that even he could not stand exposure to the radiation for more than a minute or two. But he had to discover what was causing the colossal power drain in the Systems.

The crackling sounds came from above. Staring upwards at the dim outlines of the plasma globes, he suddenly saw the clusters of pustular matter clinging to several of them, and to the interconnecting shafts. Stealthily, the Doctor emerged from hiding and inched his way towards a ladder leading up to the next level. Crouching close to the treads of the ladder, he reached the second catwalk safely and began to climb to the third level. Sections of the metalwork felt tacky, and they glistened with the familiar silver deposit. When he was halfway up the third ladder, the crackling sounds suddenly increased and the movement of the jostling, bursting bubbles quickened.

Instinctively the Doctor flung himself backwards, just as a snaking tentacle of globule lashed through the gloom towards his head. He tumbled heavily down the ladder on to the landing below. Drenched in sweat, his ears splitting from the harsh crackling and his head aching from the fall, the Doctor scrambled back into the narrow space between two reservoirs. He watched in fascinated horror as a quivering mass of greenish bubbles began to form underneath the catwalk over him, oozing through the steel mesh. It grew into a shapeless glob the size of a man, then elongated itself into a droplet. Just in time, the Doctor ducked back as it whipped out at him with a vicious crack. Missing its target, it broke into fragments which stuck to the metal rails, sizzling like hot fat a few centimetres from the Doctor's face.

He quickly looped a length of scarf round a stanchion and dived through the railings of the catwalk, swinging down to the floor. Darting through the Radiation Shield, he dragged it shut behind him and ran swiftly back to the Control Centre. The savage crackling of the globule as it had massed to attack him still filled his head. The Doctor knew that he must find some way to starve the alien creature of energy and stop it from multiplying and spreading through the Satellite; he also knew that to tamper with the Solar Plasma System could be catastrophic.

Reaching the Control Centre, the Doctor sought out the Solar Systems Panel. He stood for a moment staring at the complex displays; one slip and an irreversible chain reaction would occur. He decided that the risk had to be taken. He bent over the console and began to calculate the exact sequence in which the system would have to be run down.

'Stand away from the systems console.'

The Doctor glanced over his shoulder in surprise. He recognised Noah standing in the entrance to the Control Chamber Suite. Noah was pointing a small, torchlike weapon straight at the Doctor's head.

'Ah there you are, awake at last.' The Doctor smiled. 'I'm just about to close down the Solar Plasma Systems.'

'Move away,' said Noah. 'The Terra Nova is ours.'

'In theory certainly,' agreed the Doctor, turning back to his task. 'But unless we do something quickly, it will not be yours much longer.'

Noah advanced a few paces, levelling the weapon. 'Degenerate Seventh Colonists,' he sneered. 'Your pathetic attempt at sabotage has failed.'

The Doctor turned to face him and stood upright. He spoke rapidly but calmly. 'There is some alien life-form feeding on the energy in your Solar Reservoirs, and if we do not stop it at once it may completely overrun your Satellite.'

Noah broke into a mocking laugh. 'You and your companions are the only alien forms here,' he cried. 'It is you who must be stopped.'

There was a brilliant sheet of spark from Noah's hand. The Doctor was momentarily enveloped in a blue aura. He froze, his hand raised and his mouth half open to speak. He did not move.

4

A Fatal Wound

Full of professional admiration, Harry watched Vira moving calmly about the Cryogenic Chamber, monitoring the progress of her people as the Revivification Programme entered the final phase of its preliminary stage. From time to time, he glanced anxiously at Sarah; she did not appear to be responding to the treatment Vira had given her earlier. Vira now seemed completely oblivious of them both, and the Doctor's long absence was making Harry feel extremely uneasy. Suddenly Sarah began to moan, and her body convulsed. Harry moved to help her.

'Do not touch the female,' snapped Vira, without looking round.

'Now look here,' said Harry. 'I am a fully qualified physician and I do think I ...'

'You have no function here,' retorted Vira dismissively. 'You are intruders.'

'Charming,' muttered Harry to himself. 'If it weren't for the Doctor, neither you nor your people would be alive now.'

'The Commander will not permit contamination of the Genetic Pool,' said Vira in a hard voice. 'All Regressive influences must be eliminated.'

Harry gasped at the sinister tone of her words. At the same instant he turned, just in time to catch Sarah as she toppled forward. He eased her gently back into the pallet and checked her pulse. It fluttered weakly. He looked across at Vira, but she was totally preoccupied. All at once Sarah screamed—a terrifying hoarse cry that ripped through Harry's head. He caught her again as she staggered out of the pallet, staring with wide, panic-stricken eyes at the corpse of the giant 'locust' creature lying in the shadows. The shock brought Sarah to in a flash.

'What ... what is it ... ?' she whispered, clinging fast to Harry's arm. He was overjoyed to hear her speak, and put his arm protectively round her shoulders.

'Oh, we found it in the cupboard,' he said nonchalantly. 'Sort of galactic woodworm, old girl.'

Sarah stared around her open-mouthed. 'Where's the Doctor?' she asked shakily.

Before Harry could answer, Vira's voice pierced the quiet humming of the chamber. 'Where is Dune?' she demanded. Sarah jumped with fright. Vira was pointing to an empty pallet near where the Doctor and Harry had found the tacky trail on the chamber floor.

Sarah glanced at Harry for some explanation, but he was staring blankly at Vira as she approached them, shaking with anger. 'What have you done with Technop Dune?' she repeated. 'Answer me.' Sarah leaned heavily on Harry's arm, faint and disorientated. Her face was white, and she was trembling all over. At that moment, Noah's voice rang out over the intercom in the Access Chamber.

'Hear me, Vira ... I am in Central Control. I discovered the third Regressive attempting to sabotage the Solar Power Systems. He has been dealt with.'

'That means the Doctor,' Harry whispered as Vira hurried through into the Access Chamber.

'Commander, hear me,' they heard her say into the intercom. 'Technop Dune is missing; there is no explanation.'

'The explanation,' Noah hissed, 'is that the Regressives have taken him. Proceed with Revivification. I shall inspect the Solar Chamber ...'

Vira turned to see Harry and Sarah lingering uncertainly 'The Commander will interrogate you when he returns,' she said, brushing past them and resuming her Medtech duties.

Harry started as Sarah suddenly gripped his arm.

'Come on,' she whispered. Harry looked at her in astonishment. 'We must find the Doctor,' she said urgently.

'Well ... yes, but are you sure you're ... you're ...' Harry stammered.

Sarah smiled broadly. 'Are you all right, Harry?' she asked. 'You look a little pale.'

Harry was speechless. He shook his head in admiration at Sarah's remarkable recovery. 'You really are amazing, old girl,' he chuckled.

With a glance to check that Vira was occupied, Sarah ran lightly across the Access Chamber to the panel leading to the tunnel. 'Do you know the way to Central Control?' she whispered.

Harry pulled himself together. 'I think so ...' he muttered.

Sarah beckoned impatiently. 'Then show me how

to open this thing, and let's go,' she said.

Noah opened the Radiation Shield and entered the Solar Chamber. His movements were slow and clumsy, hampered by the heavy protective suit he now wore. At first, the thick transparent helmet muffled the vicious crackling sounds echoing round the chamber, but as Noah advanced further in, they rose to a crescendo. Noah faltered and stopped. Through the vizor he glimpsed something whipping towards his face. Restricted by the suit, he had no chance of twisting aside in time. Something caught the sleeve of his suit and gouged a deep, scorching tear. Confined inside the helmet, Noah was deafened by his own scream.

He staggered backwards down the metal ladder, the torch-shaped weapon sparking in his hand. His forearm burned beneath the gashed sleeve. He backed clumsily towards the open Shield, blinded with sweat and barely conscious. There was a hideous sensation in his injured arm, as if a column of stinging ants was forcing its way through the veins. He squeezed through the opening into the access tunnel and dragged the Shield shut. He leaned against it, gasping for breath, and tried to remove the glove from his damaged hand, but the helmet had steamed up and he could not see properly. Whimpering with pain, he fought to remove the helmet, his spasmodic breathing echoing inside it. At last the helmet came free and smashed on the tunnel floor. Noah dropped to his knees, and then slowly keeled over on his side.

His eyes bulging with terror, he brought the injured arm across in front of his face; the deep tear in the sleeve was filled with a greenish bubbling pus which, as he watched, seemed to be absorbed into his arm so that only the blackened gash in the sleeve remained. With a harsh cry Noah rolled over on to his back, the injured arm grotesquely fixed in the air. His whole body went rigid. His arm lost all sensation and he blacked out. A wisp of acrid smoke curled up from the scorched slit.

As they warily found their way to the Control Centre where Noah had reported his encounter with the Doctor, Harry did his best to explain to Sarah about the Satellite being a kind of 'Noah's Ark' bearing survivors from Earth, and how she had somehow become caught up in the works. For her part, Sarah could remember very little about her experience in the Cryogenic Suspension System, but she told Harry as much as she could.

Harry was relieved to discover that the bulkhead panels seemed to be designed to operate on a straightforward 'electric eye' mechanism when approached from the direction of the Cryogenic Chamber, and that they opened automatically.

However, there was a tense moment when he and Sarah passed through the shutter leading into the Control Centre Access Tunnel. Harry had passed through first and the shutter had closed before Sarah could join him. He waited a few moments for her to operate the photo-electric cell, but the panel remained tightly closed. Harry struggled in vain to open it by resting his forehead against the little copper plate and thinking about something complicated —just as the Doctor had done—but he did not seem able to generate the correct brain-waves. Meanwhile, Sarah had approached the 'electric eye' on the other side of the shutter, and had been startled by a sharp crackling sound behind her which made her spin round; a wobbling cluster of greenish bubbles was bursting through a grilled vent in the floor a few metres from her feet, and forming itself into threatening serpent shapes. With a shriek she had thrown herself against the panel, and as it opened, toppled white-faced into Harry's arms.

In a few seconds they reached the Control Centre. The Doctor stood smiling at them, his hand raised in greeting. 'Doctor ... you're safe,' Sarah cried, rushing over to hug him. She recoiled in horror when she realised that something was badly wrong. Harry examined the Doctor's rigid fingers. 'What's the matter with him ... ?' whispered Sarah.

'I've no idea,' said Harry, trying to bend the Doctor's arm.

'Well you're a doctor. Do something,' she cried anxiously.

Harry frowned. 'It's just as if rigor mortis ... but it can't be ...' he muttered. He put his ear to the Doctor's chest, first to the left then to the right side. 'His hearts are beating,' he said at last with relief.

Feeling very faint, Sarah sank down on the corner of the couch beside which the Doctor stood like a statue. She immediately sprang to her feet again, re-collecting her earlier experience with the Matter Transmitter. But as she leaped up she lost her balance, grabbed Harry's arm to save herself and they both collided with the Doctor, so that he fell sideways on to the couch. As he fell, his forehead touched part of the exposed electronic circuitry in the base of the couch. There was a bright flash and a popping sound. The Doctor sprang to his feet, clutching his singed forelocks.

'Ah, Sarah. How nice to see you. Splendid,' he cried. 'Where's Noah?'

'Doctor, don't you think you should sit down for a moment?' said Harry with concern.

'Sit down?' the Doctor exclaimed, staring incredulously at Harry. 'At a time like this?' He winced, and clutched his temples. 'I detest paralysators. Highly unreliable.' He looked around him. 'Where's Noah?' he repeated.

'He said he was going to examine the Solar Systems,' began Harry ...

'Quick,' cried the Doctor, striding out of the chamber. 'There might still be time to save him.'

Totally bewildered, Sarah and Harry followed. They hurried along the Cincture Structure Gallery, on their guard against the crackling, bubbling alien organism whose tracks became more and more evident.

'Strange how they've given us the run of the ship,' Harry remarked. 'Why didn't Vira try to stop us?'

'Not her function, Harry,' called the Doctor over his shoulder. 'By the Thirtieth Century, human

65

society has become highly specialised. Vira is a Med-tech; we, I suspect, are an Executive problem.'

'Correct, Doctor, but not a difficult one. You can be easily eliminated.' The snarling voice seemed to come from nowhere. They stopped in their tracks as Noah, still clad in the radiation suit, emerged without warning from an alcove in the gallery and barred their way. His left hand was held behind him, in his right he brandished the paralysator gun.

'I am delighted to see you again, Noah,' smiled the Doctor, raising his hat. 'I suggest that without more ado we put our heads together and devise a prompt solution to what is undoubtedly your most serious problem ... Unless we destroy the organism in the Solar Chamber it will ...'

Noah gestured sharply with the paralysator. 'We will return to the Cryogenic Section,' he ordered. Harry and Sarah looked at the Doctor, uncertain how he would handle this impasse. Suddenly the Doctor turned on his heel and set off along the curving gallery at a furious pace.

'You're absolutely right,' he called. 'There's not a moment to lose.'

As they entered the Cryogenic Chamber, closely followed by Noah with the paralysator still levelled at their backs, Vira was assisting a tall, blond young man out of his pallet. As soon as he saw Noah he threw up his arms in front of his face and cowered back into the alcove.

'No ... No,' he screamed, his face contorted in panic. 'Keep away ... Keep back.'

'What is wrong?' demanded Noah in a hollow

voice. The young man hid his face, trembling and whimpering. Vira looked shocked.

'I do not understand, Commander,' she murmured. 'His responses were normal.' She turned to the terrified youth. 'Libri ... it is the Commander. Commander Noah ... do you not remember?' The young man relaxed a little, and then lowered his arms.

'I ... I am sorry, Commander,' he said. 'For an instant I saw ... you were ... I saw something.'

The Doctor stepped eagerly forward. 'What did you see?' he asked.

'Silence,' Noah hissed, threatening the Doctor with the paralysator, his left hand still concealed behind him.

The Doctor looked hard at Noah. 'What have you done to your hand?' he asked calmly.

'No further warnings,' shrieked Noah hoarsely. He beckoned Libri to him. Hesitantly Libri obeyed. Noah handed him the paralysator. 'Take these Regressives to an Abeyance Unit,' he ordered. 'They will remain there until the Council has convened. If they are disruptive, eliminate them.'

Everyone stared at Noah. His harsh manner and hoarse voice contrasted violently with the restrained dignity of Vira and Libri. Vira moved towards Noah. 'Commander,' she began, 'we should not ...' but Noah ignored her.

'The Systems must be closed down. Revivification must cease at once.'

Vira and Libri exchanged shocked glances. 'Why, Commander?' said Vira in disbelief.

'It is my instruction,' Noah shrieked, his voice

breaking. 'The Programme is revised. I am Commander.'

Vira gestured round the shadowy, echoing chamber. 'Commander, the First Phase has hardly begun; we have no Technops to operate the Systems.'

'I shall operate the Systems,' snarled Noah, shuddering as some kind of spasm passed through him.

'Without First Technop Dune we cannot hope to succeed,' said Vira firmly.

'Who?' whispered Noah, trembling.

'Commander, I reported to you; Dune is missing.' Vira indicated the vacant pallet.

'You are mistaken, Vira. Dune is here.' Noah's whisper rasped and echoed around them. They stared at him. 'I am Dune,' he croaked, his face clouding as if something within him was struggling to emerge, and his conscious mind was fighting it back.

Vira suddenly moved towards him, but he backed away. 'Commander, you are injured,' she cried. 'You are unwell.'

'Yes ... No ... I ... Hear me ...' Noah faltered, his face glistening with perspiration. His body seemed twisted slightly inside the cumbersome radiation suit. 'Revivification must be discontinued now ... now ...' He backed awkwardly towards the Access Chamber, mumbling and whispering unintelligibly. All at once, with a gasp of agony, he turned his back to them. He seemed to be tearing at his injured arm. As he stumbled away through the Access Chamber he cried out, as if uttering a curse, 'No more aliens ...'

The Doctor looked straight into Libri's eyes. 'Noah must be stopped,' he said. 'There was a systems fault

68

during his Revivification—his brain is damaged.'

Vira went over and spoke to the young Medtech in an urgent whisper. 'Libri, there is no procedure for arresting Revivification. It would be fatal.'

Libri met their gaze calmly. 'Noah is our Commander,' he said.

The Doctor edged towards him. 'Can you be sure of that, Libri?' he asked. Libri flourished the paralysator at him. The Doctor stepped a little closer; Sarah caught Harry's sleeve in apprehension. The Doctor slowly took a large pocket watch from his jacket. He let it swing gently on the end of its chain in front of Libri's face. He spoke in a soft, rhythmic voice. 'Libri ... when you first saw Noah ... you had a subconscious impression ... of something horrible ... That was not your Commander ... was it?'

Libri gazed at the glittering watch, mesmerized. Then, when the Doctor finished speaking, he looked up into the Doctor's huge, piercing eyes. 'Noah must be stopped,' he cried, and rushed out of the Cryogenic Chamber in pursuit.

At once the Doctor darted across to Technop Dune's empty pallet and began poking about with the telescopic probe. Almost immediately, he took out the magnifying glass and peered through it at the end of the extended rod. 'Of course ... of course. Why didn't it occur to me before?' He strode across the chamber towards the gigantic corpse lying on the far side of the adjacent bay.

Vira swiftly overtook him, and stood in his path. 'It is not advisable for you to leave,' she warned.

The Doctor handed her the magnifier, and held up

the point of the probe to examine. Impaled on it was a fragment of colourless, rubbery membrane. 'Perhaps this will convince you that *we* are not your enemy,' he said.

Vira stared at the fragment of tissue. 'What is it?'

The Doctor knelt down, and probed about in the collapsed abdomen of the monstrous creature. 'It is almost too horrible to contemplate,' he murmured.

Completely mystified, Harry and Sarah watched over his shoulder. After a few moments, the Doctor stood up. 'As I suspected, the egg-tube is empty,' he announced. 'Egg-tube?' gasped Vira.

The Doctor gazed down at the corpse. 'The Queen Colonizer ... the Progenitor,' he said solemnly. They all stared at him. He looked round at them one by one. 'Have you heard of the Eumenes?' he asked in a hushed voice.

'It's a species of wasp,' said Harry. 'It paralyses caterpillars and lays its eggs in their corpses. When the larvae emerge they have an immediate food ...' Harry's voice trailed into silence. He looked at the Doctor in horror.

Vira put her hands to her face, speechless. Sarah covered her mouth as if she were going to be sick. The Doctor walked round them, deep in thought. 'Strange how the same life-patterns recur throughout the Galaxy ...' he mused. 'Dune was Power Systems Technician, I imagine,' he said, pausing beside Vira. She nodded. 'The larvae went straight to the Solar Stacks,' the Doctor continued. 'They absorbed Dune's knowledge, as well as his tissues.'

Vira stared across at Dune's pallet, then around the

huge chamber at the thousands of sleeping humans. Suddenly she seemed to relax. 'The Creature's larvae will perish in the Solar Chamber,' she said. 'The radiation will destroy them.'

The Doctor shook his head. 'On the contrary,' he said. 'The larval organisms are feeding on the Solar energy, and becoming more powerful every minute.'

Libri entered the Control Centre seconds behind Noah. He stood transfixed in the entrance, watching his Commander staggering about the chambers, his breath rasping and rattling, eyes rolling and body contracted into a grotesque posture. His injured arm was held up across his face, and with his other hand Noah repeatedly tore at the glove. Suddenly he stopped. Shaking his head slowly from side to side he lowered the injured arm in front of him. With a sound of water dripped into boiling fat, green pus began to bubble out through the seams of the glove, the thick material splitting like paper.

'Commander,' gasped Libri, stepping forward.

With a hideous, shrieking cry Noah reeled to face him. 'Give me the paralysator,' he croaked.

Libri backed away a pace. 'You ... you are not well, Commander,' he stammered.

Struggling to control his body, Noah advanced on him. 'I order you ...' he cried.

In his eyes Libri saw desperation and fear, and that made him hesitate for a fatal fraction of a second. Noah seized the weapon with his good hand and tried to twist it from Libri's grasp. The young Medtech stared at his leader like a hypnotised animal. Then something flew through the air and cut him across the face. He fell back, screaming and clawing at the intense burning sensation in his eyes.

Noah wrenched the paralysator from him, and pressed the trigger at point blank range. Libri's body was hurled across the chamber in a succession of frozen shapes as pulse after pulse cracked into it. When the sparking ceased, Noah stared in terror at the smouldering body of the young man welded to the panelling. Then he dragged himself through into the inner chamber, the suppurating stump of his left hand raised like a club. He hovered grotesquely over the Cryogenic Systems Panel, moaning in anguish. His right hand clung fiercely to the sleeve of the injured arm, fighting to prevent it from touching the sensitive controls ...

The chambers and tunnels of the Satellite suddenly echoed with a clear, crystal-toned chime which was followed immediately by a calm female voice. 'Greetings to the Terra Nova ... You have slept for longer than the recorded history of Humanity ... you awaken now in the dawn of a New Era ...' Noah stood immobilised in a twisted posture, his face betraying recognition of the High Minister's voice, and the shock of the returning memory of his own humanity. The voice echoed on ... 'You will return to an Earth that we cannot imagine ... a world that is dead ... You must make it flourish and live again ...'

Noah's body twisted this way and that as the human and the alien fought for supremacy within him. His mind was filled with the great purpose about which the High Minister was speaking, yet he felt himself inexorably overwhelmed by the destructive alien consciousness that was steadily possessing his mind and body. One moment he found himself listening to the High Minister's words with hope and longing for the green Earth again; then he would be seized with a dizzying sensation of dark emptiness and a fierce hate for all humans. His upright posture suddenly seemed unnatural; he stumbled forward to his knees as the voice of the High Minister, recorded thousands of years earlier, rose to an impassioned climax. He began to beat the stump of his left arm against the edge of an instrument console. The heavy protective suit seemed to be crushing the breath out of his body; he felt something within him instinctively struggling to break out as if from a shell. His alien hand hissed and crackled ...

'... and so, across the chasm of the years, I send to you the hopes of all Humanity for a safe landing ... safe landing ... safe landing ...'

The High Minister's words became an exuberant refrain in Noah's ears. He crawled across to the opening which connected the two chambers of the Control Centre, intent on vengeance against the hated Humans. He raised the paralysator, still gripped in his right hand, and directed the relentless pulses of energy at the body of the young Medtech until it had completely disintegrated into nothing. Then the weapon clattered from his grasp as Noah's human awareness gained supremacy again.

He backed into the smaller chamber, his mind struggling to overcome the urge of his injured left hand to wreck the Cryogenic Systems Panel. The arm seemed to have an existence of its own, independent of his control. As he stared at it, the sleeve suddenly split wide open, spilling out a stream of viscous matter which rapidly hardened into a glistening, cellular tissue.

It was the flesh of a Wirrrn ...

5

The Wirrrn

The Doctor and his companions stood silently as the serene voice of the High Minister flooded the Cryogenic Chamber. Vira had ascended to the second level of pallets, where the multiple humming of the Revivification process was increasing little by little as the occupants were brought gradually back to life. The Doctor had been squatting thoughtfully beside the crumbling remains of the corpse, poking about the exposed viscera of the alien creature. Harry and Sarah had been detailed to search for more of the trails left by the larvae, and to check for any other empty pallets where the creature may have laid its eggs.

'Sort of pre-match pep talk,' whispered Harry, as the High Minister drew towards the end of her message. Sarah was listening in rapt attention; she had heard the mysterious voice before, but where? Vira gazed slowly round at the ranks of her people. She could not understand what had happened to Noah, why he had ordered Revivification to cease. As she listened to the High Minister, she was filled with a renewed sense of her great mission.

The High Minister's voice was brutally interrupted by a harsh, grating whisper which broke into sudden shrieks and gasps, becoming incoherent and then lucid again. '... Vira ... Vira ... Hear me ... Expedite Revivification ... Initiate the Main Phase now ...'

Vira looked utterly bewildered. 'Noah ... Commander,' she cried, 'I do not understand ...'

'We ... you are in danger ... Take our ... your people to Earth before they ... before we ...' Noah's voice became a distorted roaring. Vira turned from side to side, staring into the dark upper reaches of the chamber as if seeking Noah there. 'They ... We are here ... in the Terra Nova,' the rasping whisper continued. 'We shall absorb the humans ... the new Earth will be ours ...'

Vira covered her face, rocking herself to and fro in terrified incomprehension.

'We are in ... Wirrrn my mind ... no time ... Libri is dead ... the Wirrrn will absorb ... Wirrrn will absorb the humans ...' The hoarse whisper of Noah's threat reverberated for some time. Then silence fell over the vast chamber.

It was broken at last by the Doctor. 'The Wirrrn ... Wirrrn ... endo-parasitism ... multi-cellular larvae ...' he muttered, as if trying to recall something from the depths of his colossal, encyclopaedic memory.

'Does that mean they'll literally eat us alive?' shuddered Sarah.

The Doctor nodded gravely. He swept his long arm in a broad gesture round the Cryogenic Chamber. 'The Revivification process is much too slow,' he warned. 'If we do not destroy the Wirrrn larvae before they develop into pupae – none of us will survive.' He crossed the chamber to the base of the elevator

76

shaft, where Vira lingered uncertainly. He took her gently by the arm. 'If we can confront Noah in time—while he still retains some vestige of his humanity—we may be able to discover a way of fighting the Wirrrn. Come.'

Vira held back. 'I cannot leave until the last of the Technop Personnel have safely revived,' she protested.

The Doctor looked earnestly into her face. 'You are the only one of us that Noah—or what is left of Noah—will trust. You must come with me—for the sake of your people.'

The Doctor quickly persuaded Harry that he had observed enough of the Revivification Process to take over from Vira for a short time, with Sarah's assistance, of course. Then he led Vira firmly out through the Access Chamber in pursuit of Noah.

As they were whisked along the Access Tunnel on the conveyor, the Doctor outlined his theory. 'I postulate a multi-nucleate organism with a shared consciousness,' he concluded. 'The larvae clustered in the Solar Chamber in order to pupate and we—first myself, then Noah —disturbed them.' They had reached the Decontamination Airlock which sealed off the Cryogenic Sector. As the shutter opened they came face to face with Noah. He was hunched in the confined space of the cubicle, still wearing the white radiation suit which was now split open down the entire left side and oozing the green, treacly bubbles of the parasite larvae. Choking fumes from the smouldering suit curled around him.

Conquering her fear and revulsion, Vira stepped

towards her Commander with outstretched arms.

'Do not touch me,' Noah rasped. His face was turned away from them, but he covered them with the paralysator.

The Doctor seized Vira's arm and pulled her behind him. He then spoke rapidly to Noah. 'Tell us one thing, Noah. How much time do we have?'

Slowly Noah turned his head fully towards them. The whole of the left side of his face was transformed into a shapeless, suppurating mass of glistening green tissue, in the midst of which his eye rolled like an enormous shelled egg. As they stared at him horrified they could almost detect the spreading movement of the alien skin.

'It ... it feels near ... very near ... now,' he croaked. As he tried to speak, a ball of crackling mucus welled out of the dark slit that was his mouth and trickled down the front of the suit. He stumbled forward. 'Vira ... Vira ...' He threw the paralysator at Vira's feet. 'For pity's sake ... kill me ... kill me now,' he pleaded, his voice barely intelligible. Then he reeled back with an appalling shriek into the airlock as, with a crack like a gigantic seed pod bursting, his whole head split open and a fountain of green froth erupted and ran sizzling down the radiation suit, burning deep trenches in the thick material. The shutter closed.

Vira stared at the closed panel, pale and shaking. 'I am sorry,' she said at last. 'I showed weakness.'

'No, I could not have done it either,' said the Doctor, picking up the weapon. 'Come, there is little time.'

For a moment Vira did not move. 'Noah ... Noah and I were pair-bonded for the new life,' she said. Her eyes were full of tears. The Doctor gently led her away, back down the Access Tunnel to the Cryogenic Chamber.

Much to their own surprise, Harry and Sarah had successfully supervised the revival of two Technops: Lycett and Rogin. At first dazed and suspicious, the technicians had soon revealed themselves to be almost friendly after Harry's and Sarah's breathless explanations. They were much less formal than Vira had been, and Rogin did not seem too surprised that things had gone wrong.

'We should have taken our chance in the Therm Shelters, and stayed on Terra Firma,' he said wistfully.

'How much Anatomy do you remember, Harry?' the Doctor cried, sweeping into the Cryogenic Chamber and going straight over to the corpse of the Wirrrn Queen.

'Quite a bit, I hope,' said Harry, joining him. 'But you'd need an Entomologist for that thing.'

Vira greeted the two Technops with obvious relief, glad to have the company of her own people again. 'We will commence Main Phase at once,' she ordered, leading them to the Access Chamber Control Suite.

'But the safety procedures ...' protested Lycett, shocked.

'We shall override them,' said Vira. 'I am Commander now, it is my decision. Take your operating stations.'

'Curious lung structure,' remarked Harry as he watched the Doctor probe through the remains of the Wirrrn Queen for some clue as to its origin and possible weaknesses.

'A superb adaptation,' the Doctor agreed. 'Its lungs recycle the creature's wastes ... almost certainly by enzymes of some kind ... carbon dioxide back to oxygen ...'

'Like plants,' suggested Sarah, craning to see.

The Doctor turned his attention to the huge head. 'Exactly, Sarah ... It seems capable of existing in Space, just occasionally visiting a planetary atmosphere for food and oxygen.'

'The way a whale rises to the surface ...' Sarah added.

The Doctor was staring at the Wirrrn's gigantic yellow eye. Suddenly he leaped to his feet and rushed through into the Access Chamber, where Vira and the two Technops were initiating the Main Phase.

'Wait,' he shouted. 'The Main Phase must wait.'

Vira turned to the Doctor in astonishment. 'But Noah said we should expedite Revivification and get our people to Earth '

The Doctor waved his arms impatiently. 'The process is much too slow,' he cried. 'The Wirrrn larvae will have pupated to imago long before the last of your people are fully revived. We may have only hours before the Wirrrn overrun the Satellite.'

Vira looked defiantly at the Doctor. She seemed to have regained her former cold authority. 'You have an alternative plan?' she challenged.

'The larvae must be entering the pupal stage now,' explained the Doctor. 'Before they develop into adult Wirrrn form, they will be relatively dormant. If we can only discover their weakness we may be able to destroy them. I wonder ...

'I need everyone's assistance,' he suddenly shouted, bolting back into the Cryogenic Chamber. For a moment nobody moved. Sarah's face lit up in anticipation as she realised the Doctor was about to launch one of his improvised experiments. For the next five minutes the Doctor rushed from one chamber to the other, issuing rapid instructions. Harry was persuaded to try his surgical skills in removing a section of the Wirrrn Queen's giant brain.

Vira reluctantly ordered Rogin and Lycett to abandon the Main Phase procedure. At first they resisted, but they grew more and more co-operative as they realised the extent of the Doctor's knowledge. They agreed to assist him in rigging up a Neural Amplification System ...

After an hour of frenzied activity, the Doctor made the final adjustments to his 'apparatus'; what looked like a lengthy piece of crochet, made out of yards of cable and connectors, hung from one of the Access Chamber Video Cabinets. Several wires stretched from the incredible tangle across to a large segment of the Wirrrn's brain tissue. The electrode terminals on the ends of the wires were inserted into various parts of the gelatinous grey substance.

Vira had stood apart from the others, looking on suspiciously while they worked. 'What are you attempting to do?' she asked sceptically as the Doctor completed his adjustments.

'In certain kinds of tissue, neural impressions can sometimes be revived by carefully controlled stimulus ...' began the Doctor.

'I've never heard of that,' Harry interrupted, frowning.

'Yes, there were theories,' said Vira in a cold, clinical voice. 'But our research was in its infancy when the Earth had to be evacuated.'

The Doctor grinned mischievously. 'Well, you see I have something of a head start in such matters.' He winked at Sarah, who winked back.

'Gypsies used to believe that the eye retained its last image after death,' she said. Vira stared at her impassively.

'Anyway, here goes,' said the Doctor, signalling to Rogin to switch in the video unit and the amplifier lash-up. 'It should at least give us an idea of the Wirrrn Queen's last moments.'

The video screen was at once mottled with white flashes of static. With great care the Doctor altered the positions of the electrode probes inserted into the Wirrrn's brain tissue. The screen showed nothing but dizzy zig-zag patterns as the Doctor connected different areas of the Wirrrn Queen's brain to his 'machine'. He sighed with disappointment.

'It's no good,' he muttered. 'The neuron matrix isn't sensitive enough. It isn't going to work.' The Doctor stared sadly at his 'crochetwork', his chin sunk on his chest.

'I am going to link in my own brain,' he announced suddenly.

Vira immediately stepped forward. 'I cannot allow it,' she cried. 'The power could burn out a living brain.' But the Doctor was already rummaging about among the circuitry.

'An ordinary brain, I agree,' came his muffled voice from inside the video cabinet. 'But mine is rather exceptional.' He grinned over his shoulder before ducking back in again.

'Doctor, it's an appallingly dangerous idea,' Harry objected.

The Doctor stood up. 'It's the only way,' he said.

The others watched apprehensively as Rogin and Lycett attached electrodes to the Doctor's temples, and connected the wires into the maze inside the cabinet and to the probes stuck into the Wirrrn brain. The Doctor pointed to the video cabinet, to the brain tissue, and then to his own head. 'Piggy in the middle,' he smiled.

Sarah shuddered. 'Do you have to do this, Doctor?' she pleaded.

Vira moved between the two Technops and the equipment. 'I forbid this,' she said. But Rogin and Lycett seemed to be fascinated by the Doctor's plan.

The Doctor gestured towards the Cryogenic Chamber, humming faintly in the background. 'The outcome of this experiment may save the Human Race,' he said. 'If it fails, then at least only the six of us will suffer.' He settled himself into one of the control console seats. 'It may be a trifle irrational of me,' he smiled, 'but humans are quite my favourite species.' Then his face grew deadly serious. 'Tie me to the chair,' he ordered.

83

The Doctor was soon secured to the seat with a variety of complicated nautical knots tied by Harry in the thick insulated wire. The Doctor told Vira to take the paralysator from his pocket. 'Do not hesitate to destroy me should anything go wrong.' Sarah looked at Harry in horror as Vira took the weapon without a word.

'Switch on,' said the Doctor. Lycett and Rogin operated a sequence of buttons. The Doctor's body shook and then arched sharply over the back of the seat. His eyes bulged out of their sockets, his mouth gaped, and he uttered a chilling gasp. Then he slumped heavily forward.

Vira moved closer to Harry and Sarah. 'He is joining his mind to the Wirrrn's,' she murmured. 'If the experiment works, he may remain part of the Wirrrn's consciousness for ever.'

Following the Doctor's instructions, Sarah and Harry, each holding an insulated electrode, systematically probed the lump of jelly-like matter from the Wirrrn's brain. Occasionally, the Doctor's limbs jerked; his head snapped suddenly upright, then lolled forward again on to his chest. On the video screen the flashes of static began to form vague shapes which dispersed and re-formed rapidly, as if some image was trying to establish itself. Sarah and Harry forced themselves to continue, despite the Doctor's agonized gasps and spasms as they moved the electrodes.

Rogin suddenly pointed to the screen. 'Look,' he cried. 'It *is* working.'

A faint, ghostly outline was steadily resolving into

a clearer and clearer picture. The Doctor uttered brief whimpering sounds, as if willing the image to become more sharply defined.

As they watched the screen with bated breaths, they heard a distant hissing and buzzing from the Cryogenic Chamber. Rogin and Lycett leaped to their feet. There was a deafening noise, like the cracking of an ice floe, followed by the sound of a damp fire crackling.

'What is that?' whispered Vira.

The two Technops rushed through into the adjacent chamber. The others remained gazing at the screen where the shadowy image had sharpened into a distinct picture of a massive Satellite revolving slowly against the heavens like a giant spinning-top. The central hub-structure was composed of a cluster of gigantic tubes, bristling with antennae and reflector dishes. The radial tunnels, or spokes, which ran outwards to the great circular rim, swelled here and there into spherical chambers and sub-structures, all inter-connected with glinting steel-lattice framework.

The Doctor sighed, as if with satisfaction. Sarah and Harry noticed that he was smiling, and rocking his head gently from side to side. On the screen the image of the Satellite was also swinging in the same rhythm. It came steadily closer until the whole screen was occupied by a close-up of a kind of entrance hatch. The Doctor began to pant, as if in anticipation. Tentacles snaked into view in the foreground of the picture and fastened themselves about the steel handholds positioned round the edge of the airlock.

'Look out, Lycett, behind you ...' came Rogin's sudden shriek from the Cryogenic Chamber. Vira spun round.

'What ... what is it ... ?' Lycett's cry of incomprehension rose to a piercing scream that rang through the chambers. For a second, Sarah and Harry stood transfixed as Lycett's cries of agony combined with the Doctor's strange moans into a grotesque medley of sounds. Then Harry sprang to life and rushed through into the Cryogenic Chamber. He caught a momentary glimpse of the glistening, bubbling creature he had seen before in the gallery. As it rolled in a great hissing ball towards him, he collided with Rogin who hurled him back into the Access Chamber and swiftly operated the shutter control. As the panel glided shut, they all watched the heaving, crackling mass wobbling across the floor towards the narrowing gap. The panel closed just in time.

'Lycett's been absorbed by the larvae ...' screamed Rogin.

Harry dived for the video console. 'Stop the experiment ... let's get out of here.'

Sarah threw herself forward, barring his way. 'No, Harry ... you could kill the Doctor if you interfere with the circuits,' she cried.

Vira gave orders in a clear, firm voice. 'Rogin: the Armoury. Bring the Laser Lances.' Rogin ran out into the Access Tunnel. Vira turned to Harry who was anxiously eyeing the grilled duct-openings set high in the walls of the Access Chamber; he knew that at any moment the larvae might burst in upon them. 'Go with Rogin,' she commanded. Harry glanced inquiringly at Sarah. She hesitated, then nodded.

'Good luck, Harry,' she said.

'And to you, old girl,' he replied, spinning round and out in pursuit of Rogin.

As the panel closed behind Harry, Sarah looked back to the video screen. The Doctor had grown strangely silent, and on the screen a blurred and bulbous image of the Control Centre had appeared. The image swung up and down, and from side to side, as if showing the view through the eyes of something which was moving slowly and awkwardly about the chamber. Suddenly, the screen whitened with a blinding glare. The image of the Control Centre reeled wildly about. Burst after burst flashed over the screen.

The Doctor began to struggle violently, fighting against the tight loops of wire which bound him to the chair, his face folded in pain. In the foreground of the picture, Sarah and Vira saw a blur of tentacle shapes flourishing defiantly. Sarah glanced from the screen to the Doctor's thrashing limbs; then she stared at the inert lump of the Wirrrn's brain tissue.

'It's the Wirrrn Queen ...' she gasped in horror, pointing to the video screen.

The Doctor uttered terrifying cries as, on the screen, the Electronic Guard discharged its lethal bolts at the Wirrrn Queen, which was now fighting its way into the second Control Chamber ... showing them all exactly what had happened in reality. Once again, the Doctor began to breathe in hoarse panting sounds; his head nodded eagerly, and his hands made rapid gripping movements in the air. As they watched, Sarah and Vira saw the tentacles come into view again; they began prising open a section of control panelling. Thick bundles of cables were ripped from their mountings. The Doctor's body became hunched, his jaw tensed open. Then, with a grotesque growling noise, he snapped his teeth shut; on the screen, severed cable-ends flew in all directions. Then the picture dissolved into static.

Sarah felt Vira's hand grip her arm sharply. She had heard it too, a distant crackling—like a bonfire at the end of a long tunnel. They stared up at the vents ...

Harry and Rogin emerged from the Armoury carrying short, rifle-like objects with dish-shaped shields fitted round the barrels. As they raced round the Cincture Structure Gallery, Rogin explained to Harry how to operate the deadly laser guns. They had to pass through the junction section where the Access Tunnel to the Solar Chambers joined the curved gallery of the Cincture Structure. As the shutter opened, they found themselves facing a monstrous apparition. Noah, his back hunched menacingly, glared at them with the huge ochre-coloured eye which occupied the whole of the left side of his head. The entire left side of his body had swollen and burst through the radiation suit, and the skin was hard and polished. In place of his left arm, three stumpy tentacles thrashed about, centimetres from their faces.

'Human fools ...' Noah's hideous croaking made the hair rise on Harry's neck. Rogin fired his laser lance at pointblank range, cutting a deep trench in Noah's glossy, shell-like body. Noah reeled back against an observation port in the outer wall of the gallery. Pressing themselves to the inner wall, Harry and Rogin inched their way through the bulkhead panel, their weapons scoring a macabre criss-cross pattern in Noah's side. They managed to slip past him, just out of reach of the knife-like hairs bristling over the jabbing tentacles.

'You ... cannot ... stop us ...' Noah croaked, turning his head as the panel began to close between them. Rogin gasped, and stopped firing as he glimpsed the still recognisable features of his Commander staring at him in agony. Then he fired a last burst of laser as the shutter slid home.

For a few seconds, Sarah and Vira had forgotten the Doctor as they stared fearfully up at the wall vents of the Access Chamber; the crackling sounds were growing louder every second, and the closed panel into the Cryogenic Chamber was beginning to vibrate like a drumskin, as if something was beating violently on the other side. Then Vira suddenly gestured in horror at the video screen. 'Dune ...' she gasped. '... Technop Dune ...' On the screen Sarah saw the image of a young man, dressed in the Tech Personnel uniform, lying helplessly in his pallet. The image came nearer and nearer. Tentacles reached out and opened the pallet shield.

Sarah struggled to calm the Doctor. His face was running with sweat and his teeth were chattering. He began to moan over and over again.

' ... Wirrrn ... Wirrrnwirrrn ... the ... Wirrrn ...'

Sarah tore the electrodes from the Doctor's head and tugged feebly at the tight knots securing him. She turned to Vira.

'Help me with him,' she implored.

Vira was staring at the blank screen. 'That ... that was Dune,' she whispered, her voice filled with shock and outrage. She looked at the Doctor's shuddering body. 'Stand away,' she ordered Sarah, who glanced up to see her levelling the paralysator directly at the Doctor.

'No ... No, you can't ...' she screamed at Vira.

'Stand away,' repeated Vira. 'The Doctor's mind has been possessed by the Wirrrn. He must be eliminated.'

Sarah threw herself at Vira and tried to wrest the weapon from her strong fingers. They struggled desperately while the Doctor remained slumped in his chair, moaning quietly as if in a trance.

'Wirrrn ... wirrrnwirr ...'

Then, from one of the grille-covered ducts above them, there erupted a mass of crackling froth. Sarah shrank down behind the Doctor's motionless body; Vira fired the paralysator at the gathering ball of larvae quivering over them. The weapon had no effect.

Sarah screamed in the Doctor's ear. 'Doctor, please help us ... help us, Doctor ...' as the crackling grew to a deafening pitch all around them. The panel sealing off the Cryogenic Chamber began to warp and shudder; round its tightly fitting edges the larvae were oozing slowly through. Vira backed away, covering Sarah and the Doctor, and firing the useless paralysator at the apparently indestructible 'creature'.

'The panel is failing,' Vira cried. The shutter folded up like melted plastic. In the entrance to the Cryogenic Chamber there hung a sizzling curtain of globules, all bursting and multiplying. Whiplash tentacles formed out of the undulating mass and flew towards them ...

6

Time Running Out

Harry and Rogin rushed into the Access Chamber just in time to slice through the fronds of larvae with the laser guns. The smouldering fragments stuck like dried glue to the floor, centimetres from Vira's feet. Raking the clustering larvae with the silent and invisible laser beams, they disintegrated the globules as easily as if they were cutting through snow with jets of water. The chamber was soon filled with a choking and sickening smoke. At once the larvae began to retreat through the ducts; the nightmarish curtain hanging in the entrance to the Cryogenic Chamber shrank away. Harry and Rogin advanced, forcing the larvae back.

The Doctor stood up, effortlessly snapping the wires that had confined him. He began to lurch towards the retreating larvae with outstretched arms.

'Doctor ... Doctor, come back,' screamed Sarah, but the Doctor stumbled heedlessly forward as if obeying some primitive instinct.

'Get back, Doctor,' shouted Harry as the Doctor crossed into his line of fire. A corner of the Doctor's jacket was sliced off by Harry's laser and fell in a smouldering spiral. Sarah had dived forward and she brought the Doctor down with an unorthodox but effective rugger tackle. He fell with a crash.

'Bravo, old girl,' yelled Harry, as he and Rogin leaped over the Doctor's prone body in pursuit of the straggling remains of the Wirrrn larvae, rapidly retreating into the Cryogenic Chamber.

For a few seconds, the Doctor lay quite still. Sarah bent over him anxiously. Vira was covering him with the paralysator. Suddenly he leaped abruptly to his feet: 'Good morning, Sarah. Is it time to get up?' he asked brightly.

Sarah hugged the Doctor, tears of relief in her eyes. 'Doctor you ... you were nearly ...' she stammered, scarcely able to speak.

The Doctor patted her on the head abstractedly, and seated himself comfortably at the control console. He took out the scorched bag of jelly-babies from his damaged pocket, prised one from the congealed mass, popped it into his mouth and offered the bag absently to Sarah. 'Breakfast?' he asked.

Sarah shook her head. 'No thanks,' she grimaced. 'They remind me too much of that larvae stuff.'

The Doctor stared at the shapeless lump of melted sweets. 'Why don't they wait?' he murmured to himself. 'In their adult form the Wirrrn will be far deadlier.'

'How many of them will there be?' said Vira. She had lowered the paralysator, but she watched the Doctor warily, still unsure of what effect the experiment might have had on him.

The Doctor chewed away thoughtfully. 'At a hatching ... perhaps a hundred ... possibly a thousand,' he said quietly. Just then, Harry and Rogin backed into the Access Chamber, covering the entrance to the

Cryogenic Chamber which was once again humming gently to itself.

'We'll be ready for them,' Harry said grimly, obviously elated by their spectacular victory with the laser guns.

The Doctor shook his head. 'The lances will be virtually useless against a swarm of fully mature Wirrrn,' he warned.

'Then how can we fight them?' said Sarah at last.

The Doctor glanced at the lump of Wirrrn brain, bristling with electrodes on the control console beside him. 'Electricity of course,' he shouted. 'I remember now—it was the electromagnetic OMDSS that killed me ... I mean the Wirrrn Queen,' he added hastily, noticing the paralysator still firmly gripped in Vira's hand.

'Yes, we saw.' Sarah pointed to the video screen.

'And you were correct, Doctor,' said Vira. 'Technop Dune was the host for the Wirrrn eggs. We saw that too.'

'But how did the Wirrrn Queen get into the Cryogenic Chamber?' asked Harry, shuddering at the recollection of the dead creature toppling out on him.

'The most tenacious willpower,' replied the Doctor. 'I could feel it fighting off death until it had spawned; until its task was completed.'

He stood up, stuffing the sweets back into his coat. 'We must get back to the Control Centre,' he said. 'There should be some way of electrifying the Infrastructure and the Solar Chamber from there.' He strode towards the entrance to the Access Tunnel.

'Noah's out there,' Harry cried, barring the Doctor's way. He quickly related their recent encounter with Noah.

The Doctor slapped his forehead. 'Of course,' he said. '*That's* why the larvae emerged *now*; they can bypass the pupal stage by taking over fully conscious living tissue—like Noah's body. That way they can accelerate the transformation into mature Wirrrn form.' He glanced towards the Cryogenic Chamber. The panel lay buckled beside the entrance. 'We've won a breathing space, but we're trapped.' His eyes roved around the Access Chamber, seeking inspiration. 'We've got to reach the Control Centre.'

The Doctor's darting gaze lighted on the Matter Transmitter Couch. He smiled at his companions. 'Now that little gadget can be made to go backwards.'

Rogin shook his head. 'To reverse the polarities would take us hours, Doctor,' he objected. 'There just is not time.'

The Doctor tapped the side of his head. 'It so happens that I have a few short-cut methods of my own,' he said, diving under the control console of the Matter Transmitter.

Rogin looked round unhappily at the others. 'But if there should be the slightest error . . .' he began.

'Take your choice,' came the Doctor's muffled interruption. '. . . If this little trick fails, we shall either be gobbled up by the Wirrrn, or dispersed particle by particle into infinity. And I know which of the two fates I should prefer,' he added, re-emerging from beneath the console and touching a switch.

The transparent shroud covering the couch slid smoothly aside. The Doctor motioned Rogin to climb

95

on to it. 'After you,' he smiled. With a moment's hesitation and a reluctant nod of assent from Vira, Rogin gripped his laser gun firmly and lay down on the couch. The shroud slid shut. The Doctor pressed a series of switches; Rogin faded to a ghostly outline and then disappeared. Harry's eyes were almost popping out of his head.

'You next, Harry,' said the Doctor. In a daze Harry obeyed. He too faded and disappeared. As Sarah took her turn, the Doctor muttered confidentially to her, 'Sarah, I'm so relieved—I was not at all sure it would work.'

Sarah smiled nervously. 'Here I go again,' she called as the shroud closed over her.

The Doctor operated the switches; Sarah became a ghost for a moment and then returned to flesh and blood reality. Through the transparent shroud she grimaced at the Doctor. He smiled apologetically and tried again. Sarah faded a second time and instantly reappeared.

At the same moment, the lights in the Access Chamber flickered and sank to a mere glimmer. Rogin's voice crackled feebly over the intercom from the Control Centre. 'Commander, we have a power fade in Section Three.'

Vira pointed to a warning display on a nearby console. 'The Oxygen System has ceased operation,' she murmured.

The Doctor beat his fists together in frustration. 'We're so helpless in here,' he cried. 'If we could only dispose of Noah we might have a chance of tackling the larvae while they are still in the chrysalis stage—

assuming that they are by now.' He glanced up at the vents. An urgent tapping reminded him that Sarah was still trapped in the Matter Transmitter Couch at his side.

'Obviously I'm not going anywhere,' she scowled as the Doctor released her. 'Where are *you* going though?' she demanded as the Doctor suddenly whirled round and made for the Access Tunnel.

'I shan't be long,' he called. 'Lock the door behind me—and don't let any*one* or any*thing* in.'

'Doctor,' Sarah shouted vainly after him, 'Noah is out there and you . . .'

But he was gone.

Every nerve taut, his senses as sharp as those of a wild beast stalking its prey, the Doctor sped through the dark, empty tunnels. At any moment he might encounter Noah or the larvae, and he had no weapon with which to defend himself. Although Sarah and Vira were armed with the paralysator and with a laser lance, he knew they were in terrible danger every moment he was away from the Access Chamber.

He soon reached the Radiation Shield leading into the Solar Chamber. The shattered helmet belonging to Noah's protective suit still lay where it had fallen. With great care the Doctor opened the Shield and stepped warily into the Solar Chamber. At first he thought the chamber was deserted. He was about to switch on the torch to make sure, when he suddenly noticed that clinging to the softly glowing reservoirs of the upper levels were huge, ovoid crystalline objects. 'The pupal stage . . .' he breathed, peering up into the gloom. Every fibre alert, he advanced up the steel ladder to the first level of reservoirs. The Wirrrn pupae were transparent—like huge lumps of clouded glass—inside which the skeletal form of the adult Wirrrn was clearly visible, pulsating rhythmically like a heartbeat.

Stealthily the Doctor approached the broad centre shaft which contained the Solar Chamber systems controls and displays. He found the Section Three panel open, its interior totally wrecked. He set to work to try and salvage the oxygen supply circuits, at the same time forming in his mind a scheme to electrify the Solar Chamber and thus prevent the adult Wirrrn from breaking out once they reached the imago stage. An occasional sharp splitting sound came from the massed pupae above him, and the chamber was filled with subdued rustlings and movements as the Wirrrn chrysali absorbed energy from the globes.

A shrill rattle, like the sound of a giant cicada, made the Doctor spin round. A Wirrrn hovered over him, scraps of radiation suit still clinging to its body.

'Noah,' gasped the Doctor, pressing himself against the exposed circuits. The eerie rattling was made by the rows of scythe-like hairs rubbing together. The Wirrrn turned first one, then the other of its huge eyes towards him. Then, with a sudden contortion of its segmented body, it brought its tail up and over its head so that the murderous claw hung above the Doctor like the sting of a giant scorpion. The shrill rattling reached a climax as the claw opened. The creature seemed to purr with triumph, uttering its own name. 'Wirrrrrrrrrrrrrrrn ...'

The vicious claw swung down at the Doctor's throat.

Suddenly a series of deep lines was scored across the underbelly of the rearing Wirrrn. It turned from the Doctor to face the attack. From somewhere below him, the Doctor heard Sarah screaming. 'Run, Doctor. *Run* ...' He threw himself between the creature's razor-bristling legs and rolled across the steel landing. He glimpsed the terrified faces of Sarah and Vira in the torch-beam. They were pointing the paralysator and the laser lance uncertainly into the half-light. The Doctor dived down the companionway.

'Get out. Out. Both of you,' he roared. 'The radiation in here could kill you.' Reaching them, and grabbing them by the arms, he steered them towards the open Shield and safety.

'Stay, Vira, stay ...' The words seemed to come from the depths of the chamber itself rather than from the hideous apparition before them. Vira twisted free from the Doctor's grasp and turned, letting go the laser lance which fell clattering into the darkness below them.

'Noah ... Commander ...' Vira cried, her voice choked with tears.

The Wirrrn moved gradually closer to them, its legs rustling like dry leaves against the metal struts. It stopped a few metres away, crouched on the edge of the gantry above them.

'Abandon the Satellite now ... Take the Transport Vessel ... If you remain you will perish with the Sleepers. ...' The hushed whisper enfolded them like a breeze. It was just recognisably the voice of Noah, but it issued from the huge quivering mandibles of the giant insect looming over them.

Vira tried to approach a step nearer, but the Doctor held her firmly back. 'We cannot abandon the Terra Nova. You know that,' she murmured.

The creature reared up again, its tentacles bristling. 'The Wirrrn must survive ... When we emerge the humans will be destroyed—just as they destroyed us ...'

'What does he mean?' whispered Sarah.

Noah reached out over them with quivering tentacles. 'Humans came to Andromeda ... For long ages the Wirrrn fought them ... But they destroyed our breeding colonies on Andromeda Gamma Epsilon ...'

Vira turned to the Doctor with shining eyes. 'Then our stellar pioneers succeeded,' she whispered.

'... Since that time the Wirrrn have searched the Emptiness for new breeding places ... Now we have found an ideal habitat ... The Satellite is ours ...'

The Doctor edged forward a little. 'The Wirrrn inhabit the Emptiness,' he said quietly. 'They do not need the Satellite.' Noah was poised over them like a gigantic preying mantis.

'You know nothing,' he rasped. 'Our breeding is terrestrial—we require hosts for our hatchings ... We shall use the humans in the Cryogenic Chamber ... In one generation the Wirrrn will become an advanced technological species ... We shall ...' A sharp splitting sound obliterated the rest of Noah's words. The Doctor eased the two women slowly back towards the entrance.

'The pupae are beginning to open,' he muttered. 'It's time we were leaving.'

As he spoke there came a fusillade of splitting sounds in rapid succession. The Wirrrn's head moved slowly from side to side, staring at them with fathomless, glowing eyes. Its claw swung in the darkness above them. 'Leave the Satellite, Vira ... Leave now ...'

Vira tried to resist the Doctor's guiding hand. 'Noah ... Noah,' she faltered.

A shattering crescendo of cracks like gunfire made the Doctor whirl round and thrust Sarah and Vira out into the tunnel. He closed the Shield manually, and whipping out the sonic screwdriver, directed it at the locking panel for a few seconds. 'That should scramble the works,' he said. 'They'll have to chew their way out now.' Then he led his two companions into the pitch darkness of the labyrinthine Satellite ...

Harry stared down at the Matter Transmitter Couch in the Control Centre where, for the past ten minutes, he had expected the others to materialise just as he and Rogin had done. 'Something's gone wrong with this gadget,' he said gloomily.

Rogin grunted. He was busy working on a set of systems panels he had lifted out from the wall. He had succeeded in restoring the lighting in the Control Chambers although it was not very bright.

Harry was irritated by the Technop's apparent lack of concern. 'Well, I do think we ought at least to investigate,' he said.

Rogin pointed out that there was no lighting else-where in the Terra Nova. 'After what happened to Lycett,' he added, 'I want to see where I am treading.'

Harry glanced down at his own shoeless feet. '*You* should worry,' he muttered.

'Still no oxygen,' said Rogin, shaking his head. He stood up, and as he did so seemed to jump a little from the floor and to be suspended for a fraction of a second in the air. At the same moment, Harry realised that the laser lance he was holding appeared to have be-come mysteriously lighter. Before he could remark on it, there came a sudden clatter from the adjacent Control Chamber, where the TARDIS had mater-ialised. Rogin grabbed the lance from Harry and con-cealed himself to one side of the opening into the neighbouring chamber. Harry leaped to the other side, bouncing lightly across the floor.

'Anyone at home?' The Doctor's hat was poked through the open panel and waved about on the end of the telescopic probe.

'Where on earth have you all been?' cried Harry as the Doctor entered, followed by Sarah and Vira.

'We bumped into Noah,' Sarah said wryly.

'Excellent work, Rogin,' the Doctor said approv-ingly. 'You've managed to shed a little bit of light on our problems.'

'I have diverted power from the Gravity Static Field, Doctor,' explained Rogin.

'I thought I was feeling rather light-headed,' Sarah joked half-heartedly. Rogin explained that he had not been able to restore the oxygen systems. Vira hurried over to the Cryogenic Systems Monitor Panel. The

Doctor perched on the edge of the Transmitter Couch and silently offered round the bag of melted jelly-babies. No one responded. He sat deep in thought.

The silence soon became unbearable.

'Perhaps we should take Noah's advice,' said Sarah.

'And what was that?' Harry asked.

'Vamoose, or stick around and be killed,' she replied.

Harry at once moved towards the entrance. 'Well I'm certainly ready to get going,' he said eagerly. 'Why don't we all jump into the TARDIS?'

'Vira has no intention of abandoning her people, and neither have we,' the Doctor snapped.

Sarah moved over to join Harry. 'So that settles *us*,' she sighed. 'We'll just stay here and suffocate, or freeze or be gobbled up.'

With a cry of frustration the Doctor leaped up. 'If we only had a power source we could electrify the bulkheads of the Cryogenic Section ... The Wirrrn would never get through,' he said. '... There must be a way—even with Noah in control of the Solar Chamber.'

At that moment, Sarah remembered something. 'Just a minute,' she cried, 'Noah said ...'

Harry interrupted her. 'Perhaps we could lure Noah out of the Infrastructure and into a trap,' he suggested.

'What do you have in mind, Harry?' the Doctor asked cuttingly. '... a concealed trench covered with elephant grass?'

Sarah tried to gain their attention. 'Doctor, listen, I've just remembered ...'

The Doctor held up his hand for silence. He turned to Rogin. 'Could we confuse the Wirrrn by altering the Gravity Static Field?' he asked.

The Technop shook his head. 'It would take hours to trace the lines of force,' he objected. The Doctor nodded in professional agreement.

'Will someone please listen to me?' Sarah had climbed up on to the couch and was waving her arms frantically in the air. The Doctor rounded on her with barely concealed annoyance.

'What is it, Sarah?' he demanded sharply.

'Noah mentioned a Transporter Vessel,' she replied. They all looked blankly at her. 'Well, presumably it has a power system of its own ...'

The Doctor clutched at his head. 'Why didn't you mention this before?' he cried. 'I can't be expected to think of everything, you know,' he added with a grieved expression.

Harry helped Sarah down from the couch. 'Well done, old girl,' he grinned.

The Doctor rubbed his hands together with renewed spirit. He asked Rogin how to reach the Transport Vessel. Rogin leaned across and activated a large display-plan of the entire Satellite. He indicated a shortened 'spoke' leading from the Cincture Structure towards the central Infrastructure or 'hub', and ending halfway in a circular Docking Structure where the Transport Vessel was mounted. The Doctor studied the display closely.

'We would have to run cables halfway round the Cincture Structure from the Transport Vessel to the Cryogenic Chamber,' he murmured doubtfully. 'The

104

Wirrrn will simply cut them.' Rogin nodded. The Doctor leaned closer to the illuminated plan. 'What are those?' He indicated a complex of shafts and lattice girders joining the Transporter Dock to the Central Hub where the Cryogenic Section was housed.

Rogin shrugged. 'Obsolete structures,' he said. 'Relics of the time when the Satellite was functioning as a research base for stellar exploration.'

The Doctor peered through his magnifying glass. 'They connect the Transporter Dock with the Cryogenic Section,' he said excitedly.

'It is possible,' agreed Rogin. 'But we would require a mechanical cable-runner; the conduits are only forty centimetres square.'

There was a silence. Vira crossed the chamber from the Cryogenic Systems Panel. 'We must do something soon,' she murmured.

'Couldn't I take the cable through?' suggested Sarah. 'I don't take up much room.'

'That's no job for you, Sarah,' Harry said firmly.

Sarah flushed with indignation. 'Now look here, Doctor Sullivan . . .' she began.

The Doctor held out a length of his scarf in front of him, and moving his hands apart, he counted off the coloured stripes. 'There: forty centimetres,' he said, looking earnestly at Sarah. '. . . Do you think you could crawl through a shaft only this wide?'

Sarah looked at the short length of scarf stretched between the Doctor's hands, and then glanced round at the others with a cool, determined air. If she was having second thoughts she was certainly not going to admit it. 'Of course I could,' she declared firmly. The

Doctor was full of admiration for her courage, but he looked worried. He explained that there would be very little air or heat in the shafts, and that Sarah would have no shielding against cosmic radiation from Space. He also warned her that there would probably be many dead-ends and confusing junctions.

There was a short silence. Harry was looking apprehensively at Sarah and shaking his head. That was enough for Sarah; she thrust her chin defiantly forward. 'Well, what are we waiting for?' she cried. 'We'd better get started at once.'

The Doctor hesitated a moment, then he patted her shoulder and nodded. 'Splendid, Miss Smith,' he said. 'At last—an assignment worthy of your talents . . .'

They swiftly made their way from the Control Centre to the great wheel-shaped Cincture Structure, the Doctor's torch playing eerily over the polished walls of the tunnels. Everywhere was dark, silent and airless. The immobilised shutters were opened by means of small electronic master keys carried by Rogin and Vira. The curved gallery of the Cincture Structure was dimly lit by the glimmering stars shining through the observation portals. In every shadowed alcove and corner they expected to find the Wirrrn waiting for them; but the Satellite appeared deserted. Here and there the torch picked out the silver tracks of the Wirrrn larvae, and Sarah shuddered when they came upon blackened scraps of Noah's protective suit littering the gallery floor.

When they reached the junction with the Cryogenic Access Tunnel, the Doctor parted company with the others. Giving the thumbs-up sign to Sarah, he entered the Decontamination Airlock. 'It shouldn't take me long to wire up the Cryogenic Chamber,' he whispered. 'I'll be ready by the time you bring the cable through, Sarah. Good luck, everyone.' The Doctor waved, and disappeared.

Rogin led Sarah, Harry and Vira further on round the Cincture Structure towards the Transporter Dock Access Tunnel ... They all knew that Sarah was about to risk her life in an appallingly dangerous mission. Sarah herself knew that for a journalist it was the scoop of a lifetime; but above all else in her mind was the realisation that the future of the entire human race might now depend upon her success ...

7

A Tight Squeeze

In the centre of the Solar Chamber hovered Noah, awaiting the final metamorphosis of the Wirrrn creatures. The chamber was seething with nightmarish activity as the pupae began to split asunder to allow the emergence of the fully developed Wirrrn. First, the transparent crystalline pods became clouded and opaque as billions of tiny fissures burst through the brittle, resinous tissue. Then the pods began to disintegrate and flake apart as the creatures within pushed their tentacles through, sawing their way out with the sharp, bristling hairs. Unearthly shrieks and whistlings echoed round the chamber as the adult Wirrrn struggled to shed their crumbling pupal form. In the midst of the upheaval Noah was poised, with raised antennae, to establish himself as swarm leader . . .

Rogin and his party reached the Dock Section safely. They entered, through a complex of airlocks, into a dish-shaped area about thirty metres across. Enormous bell-shaped nozzles hung overhead, and the cradle supporting the Transport Vessel enclosed the humans in a thicket of light steel struts. The Transporter itself towered invisibly above them. Rogin at once began to clamber up one of the support struts towards a small maintenance hatch set in the underside of the Transporter. He carried one end of a heavy high-tension cable from a vast coil that he and Harry had manhandled from an equipment bay.

Vira led Sarah over to a series of small sealed openings in the side of the 'dish' area. She opened several of them with the electronic master key, and directed a powerful microlamp into the dark conduits. 'This one might be possible.' She motioned Sarah to look. The shaft was just sufficiently wide to accommodate Sarah's hunched shoulders.

'It's awfully narrow, old girl,' muttered Harry, peering into the icy darkness. '... If you take a wrong turning, I doubt whether you'll be able to turn back.'

Sarah smiled bravely. 'Then I'll just have to make sure that I don't, won't I?'

Vira helped Sarah to fit a tiny two-way communicator, designed rather like a hearing aid with microphone attached, into her ear. Harry unravelled the other end of the cable that Rogin was busy connecting into the Transporter's generators, and secured it tightly round Sarah's waist with a complicated nautical knot.

'Well, it would be an awful bore if it came undone,' he said, as Sarah tugged frantically at the loop of cable to gain a little room to breathe.

'Let's hope it's long enough,' she gasped. Vira quickly explained to Sarah how she would be guided through the conduits by radio from the Transporter Control Deck. She clasped Sarah's hand in a brief gesture of good luck and clambered up to join Rogin in the Transporter Vessel ...

When all was ready, Harry assisted Sarah as she squeezed herself into the conduit, and began to pay out the cable as she inched her way into the darkness. After a few metres, the cable stopped moving. Harry poked his head into the narrow opening. 'How are you doing, Sarah?' he called.

'. . . 've harly go starhed yet . . .' came the muffled reply.

'Sorry, old girl. I thought you were stuck,' Harry shouted. At once the cable was jerked sharply out of his hands. Harry smiled to himself.

'Jolly good luck, old thing,' he murmured.

In the Cryogenic Chamber the Doctor was well advanced with the task of welding cable terminals to the wall sections of the huge vault. All around him, the sleeping survivors of a terrestrial catastrophe lay suspended between life and death, the delicate Revivification systems starved of vital power, and the threat of the rapidly developing Wirrrn hanging over them. If Sarah succeeded in reaching the Cryogenic Chamber with the power cable, then there was a good chance of not only preventing the Wirrrn from invading the chamber, but also of restoring power to the chamber's vital systems.

Suddenly the Doctor switched off the torch and thrust the sonic screwdriver back into his pocket. He stood quite still, barely breathing, listening intently. There was a faint, dry rustling sound; then silence. He peered into the darkness. In the direction of the Access Chamber he saw two huge, ochre globes swinging from side to side: the eyes of a Wirrrn. He backed stealthily away until he felt the outline of a pallet behind him. Without taking his eyes from the baleful stare of the creature he opened the shield. To his relief he found that the pallet was empty. He climbed inside and closed the shield. He lay motionless, straining his eyes to see through the thick, distorting material ...

The Wirrrn moved slowly round the perimeter of the chamber, apparently pausing to examine some of the pallets. Eventually it approached and stopped in front of the Doctor, turning first one and then the other eye towards him. The Doctor started, just managing to suppress a cry, as something rattled and scraped against the pallet shield. He blinked the sweat out of his eyes, and fought against the painful cramp caused by his keeping utterly still in such an awkward posture. The Wirrrn seemed to stare in at him for an eternity, its sharp spines scratching against the shield with a noise that set his teeth on edge. Then abruptly it turned away, and crawled across the chamber towards the remains of the Wirrrn Queen. The Doctor pressed his face against the pallet shield. He could just make out the faint image of the Wirrrn's eyes as the creature whirled in a frenzy away from the huge corpse of its progenitor, and disappeared whence it had come.

The Doctor waited for a few minutes, then quietly raised the shield and climbed out of the pallet ...

As Harry clambered laboriously into the Control

Module of the Transporter, he overheard Rogin speaking quietly to Vira. '... everything is perfect, Commander. We could depart for Earth now. There is nothing to stop us ...'

'I say, just a minute ...' said Harry suspiciously, easing himself up into the small, cramped chamber. Rogin and Vira were seated in moving, padded chairs which slid along and revolved around a slim steel pillar running the length of the cylindrical chamber, thus allowing the occupants to reach all parts of the control panelling.

'Generator Manual Overrides linked, Commander,' announced Rogin, completely ignoring Harry. 'Initiation of Primary Phasing in forty-five seconds from now.'

At that moment, Sarah's voice burst loudly over the intercom. 'Hello, Rogin. I've reached what feels like a three way junction ... it's very tight ...'

Rogin traced his finger over an illuminated plan of the conduit structure on the video-screen before him. 'You are making good progress,' he replied. 'You must now proceed to the left.' There was a short silence, broken by the sound of Sarah's struggling efforts.

'I can ... I can hardly move at all ...' she suddenly panted. There was the sound of a brief tussle, and then Sarah's frightened whisper. 'I think the cable is caught somehow ...'

Vira swung angrily round on Harry. 'You should not have left the conduit hatch,' she said icily. 'The cable is obstructed.'

Harry shamefacedly scrambled back down the alloy ladder, and descended swiftly to the Docking Area.

Inside the conduit, Sarah was drenched in perspiration despite the intense coldness which numbed her fingers. She had to fight for every breath. Her knees and elbows were raw from scraping against the sides of the narrow shafts. Her hair repeatedly caught itself between her shoulders and the metal sides of the conduits, forcing her to continually retreat a few centimetres in order to release it. The smooth sides afforded her nothing to grip on. She could move only with a kind of caterpillar action which was terribly exhausting; she contracted her body, pressed her knees against the shaft and then straightened her body, pressed her elbows outwards and finally drew her legs along after her by contracting her body. She had to repeat this awkward sequence over and over again. She was often close to despair as the cable snagged, or the bulky knot which Harry had tied jammed itself between her hip and the side of the shaft.

Now she was twisting this way and that in a frantic attempt to free the cable; but it refused to budge, and the more Sarah wriggled, the tighter she became stuck. Tears of frustration welled up in her eyes. Her skin seemed to adhere to the cold metal shaft, and would only come away with a sharp and painful wrench. She could see absolutely nothing. She gasped for oxygen. She could move neither forwards nor backwards. 'It's just no good ...' she sobbed. 'I'm sorry, I can't do anything to ...'

All at once she felt the cable tugging. For a horrifying moment she thought that something was in the shaft with her, and trying to drag her back towards itself. She had a fleeting vision of the Wirrrn larvae bubbling up through the shaft and engulfing her in a searing, suffocating mass. Then she realised that the jerking of the cable formed a regular pattern; it seemed like a morse code message! After a few minutes concentration she deciphered it: 'COME ON OLD GIRL ... YOU CAN DO IT.' Instantly Sarah's energy increased a hundredfold. 'Patronising male chauvinist,' she muttered through clenched teeth, visualising Harry's anxious face at the other end of the conduit.

With a supreme effort she eased herself forward a few centimetres. To her amazement and joy the cable did not resist. 'Just ... you wait ... till I get out ...' she panted.

'Please repeat your last message,' requested Rogin's puzzled voice over the communicator.

Sarah heaved herself forward. 'Message cancelled,' she replied. At once she was confronted by a bewildering array of shafts branching off in all directions. Even following Rogin's careful instructions, it was almost impossible to orientate oneself in the pitch darkness. Sarah knew that if she took a wrong tunnel, or came to a dead end, she had no chance of making her way back again.

A faint glimmer of light ahead spurred her on. 'I can see light,' she whispered excitedly into the tiny microphone.

'Yes,' came Rogin's encouraging reply. 'You are entering an old Hydrodynamics System. It runs right through the Solar Chamber—move as quietly as you can.' To her horror, Sarah found that the conduit had become tubular in section, and even narrower than before. She now had to stretch out her arms ahead of her, and to move forward by turning her whole body like a corkscrew. She ceased to be aware of her badly grazed elbows and knees, of the burning sensation in her lungs, but forced herself onward through the tube. Her painfully slow progress was further hampered by her legs becoming inextricably tangled with the cable as she rotated her body.

She soon found herself in a section constructed of translucent material. Her pounding heart missed a beat as she recognised, through the thick glass-like material, the subdued glow of the Solar Chamber. Rogin's voice came whispering through the earpiece; it seemed to come from the other side of the universe. 'Quietly now, Sarah ...'

She froze as, from the depths of the Solar Chamber, there loomed two enormous eyes. Helplessly Sarah stared back at the Wirrrn crawling towards her, its gigantic mandibles working hungrily. The creature gripped the tube with its tentacles. In vain Sarah tried to flinch away from the slashing, razor hairs as they squeaked against the conduit only centimetres from her body.

The Wirrrn tried to take the tube between its mandibles. Sarah could see right into the dark red pulsing throat of the giant insect. She felt violently sick. Rogin's voice came urgently over the communicator. 'Sarah ... what is happening ... are you safe?'

The inside of the tube had steamed up so that

Sarah could no longer see her attacker, but only hear the shrill scrape of its tentacles, and feel the shuddering of the tube as the Wirrrn tried to crush it. She marvelled at the extraordinary strength of the unfamiliar glassy substance which was all that kept her from the jaws of the creature. She felt like a fly trapped in a blob of amber which could at any moment be smashed to smithereens with a hammer.

She collected her wits, and frantically twisted herself along the tube. The Wirrrn followed, angrily wrenching at the conduit, its eyes burning at her through the tubing and its massive jaws completely enclosing her struggling body. Sarah glimpsed more and more of the fierce glowing eyes clustering around her as she fought her way through the final section of the Solar Chamber ... She imagined herself crawling through the bowels of some prodigious mythical beast.

To her relief, the tube suddenly reverted to metal sections. She welcomed the darkness with its feeling of security, but she could not be sure that the Wirrrn would not eventually manage to shatter the 'glass' section and sever the vital cable—or even drag her backwards into the Solar Chamber again.

'Is ... is it much further ... ?' she implored, her imagination conjuring an endless maze of dark, stifling tunnels in which she was condemned to crawl for ever.

'You are almost there ... another fifteen metres,' came Rogin's welcome reply.

'I do hope so ...' Sarah gasped, '... because I don't think I can go on much longer.'

'Stick at it, old girl,' came Harry's cheerful voice.

'That's just the trouble,' Sarah snapped back. 'I keep getting stuck.' Then she managed a smile to herself as she visualised Vira's and Rogin's blank stares on hearing her little joke.

The Doctor had almost completed his preparations in the Cryogenic Chamber. For the moment, the Wirrrn seemed to be leaving him in peace, deterred perhaps by the discovery of the corpse of the Queen. Nevertheless, the Doctor remained fully alert as he crouched in the darkness, sonic-welding cables from the wall terminals into a large junction box by torchlight. From time to time, he crossed to the central shaft and listened for signs of Sarah's progress. It was nearly an hour since he had bid her good luck in the Cincture Structure. He knew that it could not be very long before the Wirrrn in the Solar Chamber reached imago form in overwhelming numbers, and returned to the attack.

There was a hollow, distant panting sound which suddenly reverberated in the central shaft. The Doctor raced across the chamber into the elevator cubicle where the Wirrrn Queen had been hidden, and put his ear to the side of the shaft.

'Sarah ...' he murmured. He tapped rhythmically and then listened. His tapping was repeated beat for beat. 'Sarah ... Hurry, Sarah ... hurry,' he called, shining his torch up into the darkness. Ducts and conduits ran into the shaft at right angles as far as the Doctor could see. He directed the torch-beam at each aperture in turn. 'Can you see anything, my dear?' he said. There was a pause, then Sarah's faint reply.

'No ... not yet. I'm now in some kind of coiled section, Doctor. I'm not sure I can get round the bends ...'

'Of course you can, Sarah,' encouraged the Doctor, keeping a wary eye on the dark vault of the Cryogenic Chamber. 'You've got this far ...'

'But, Doctor, I'm completely stuck this time,' Sarah whimpered. '... I seem to be glued to the sides.' The tall shaft rang with Sarah's sobs of frustration and fear. 'Doctor, I'm ... I'm upside down ... and I feel very very faint ...'

The Doctor stared upwards, his face full of anxiety. They were so close to succeeding. Sarah could not fail now. He cupped his hands to his mouth and bellowed as loudly as he could up into the shadows. 'That's right ... blubber away, Sarah ... just what I expected of you.'

There was a brief pause, then Sarah protested tearfully, 'But, Doctor, I am completely jammed. I can't go up or down.'

'Oh, stop whining, girl,' retorted the Doctor brutally. 'You are utterly useless.'

There was a shocked silence. 'Doctor,' Sarah's voice came through at last. 'Doctor, how can you ...'

But the Doctor showed no remorse. Instead of apologising he went on, 'It was a mistake to rely on you in the first place ... Harry was quite right—— It was no job for a girl ...'

Sarah had heard enough. She wrenched herself round and round inside the tortuous spiralling tube in a frenzy, oblivious of pain, fear or discomfort. 'You wait ... I'll show you ...' she gasped.

The Doctor was smiling broadly to himself, delighted that his little ruse had worked so well. 'The future of Mankind at stake, and all you can do is lie there blubbering,' he called as a final goad to Sarah's temper.

But Sarah was no longer listening. Within a few minutes her head appeared out of one of the ducts high up in the shaft wall. In the torchlight the Doctor could see that her hair was matted and her face streaked with tears, but her smile was triumphant.

The Doctor grinned up at her. 'Splendid, Sarah. I knew you would do it,' he whispered.

Sarah peered down at him in amazement, dazzled by the torch. Then she smiled again. 'You are a brute,' she laughed, despite her exhaustion. 'You conned me completely.'

'Just trying to encourage you, my dear, that's all,' the Doctor murmured innocently. He shone the torch around the sides of the shaft. Sarah was stranded a good thirty metres above him. 'Now all we have to do is get you down,' he said.

'Oh, please don't worry about me. I'll just jump,' retorted Sarah. 'As long as you get the cable down safely I'm sure I hardly matter.'

The Doctor swept the torch round the cubicle. 'If we had any power I could fetch you down in the lift,' he said.

There came a sharp rattling sound from the Access Chamber. Instantly the Doctor began working away with the two lengths of his scarf. Sarah could not see what he was doing, but she gasped in astonishment and admiration when, after a few seconds, he flashed the torch quickly over the giant 'cat's cradle' he had fashioned across the bottom of the shaft, using the framework of the open elevator cubicle on which to secure the scarf-ends.

'Jump, Sarah, jump,' the Doctor hissed.

Without pausing to think, Sarah obeyed and leaped into the dark abyss. She landed in the safety-net the Doctor had improvised. A pair of strong hands came out of the darkness and lifted her gently but quickly down.

'Harry's tied the Gordian Knot here all right,' whispered the Doctor, feverishly trying to undo the cable from around Sarah's waist.

Over the Doctor's shoulder, Sarah suddenly noticed the unmistakable glow of a Wirrrn's eyes on the far side of the Cryogenic Chamber. Only minutes earlier she had been struggling between the jaws of one of the fearsome creatures inside the conduit. A violent shudder shook her body and she thrust her fingers into her mouth to stifle a scream. At the same moment, the Doctor freed the cable. Something was pushed into her free hand. It was the torch. 'Try to distract it, Sarah,' murmured the Doctor, moving stealthily away from her with the cable.

'What ... ?' she gasped. But there was no time to protest.

She switched on the torch and shone the beam up over her face from under her chin, transforming her features into a macabre mask suspended in mid-air. She felt the Doctor detach the communicator set from around her head.

'Splendid idea,' prompted his voice in her ear. 'But whatever you do, keep away from the walls.'

Sarah began to sidestep away from the Doctor, her eyes fixed firmly on those of the Wirrrn. The huge, ochre globes swung steadily towards her; she could hear the heavy, leathery body dragging itself across the chamber floor as she backed away from it. Still very dazed from her ordeal inside the conduit system, Sarah struggled to visualise the exact shape of the Cryogenic Chamber so that she would not back into any of the walls; she knew that hundreds of thousands of volts would surge through them when Rogin switched on the power. She could just make out the Doctor's whispered instructions to Rogin through the communicator. Counting her faltering steps, Sarah knew she must be very close to the chamber wall. Still the Wirrrn bore down upon her.

Suddenly, to her left, she heard the Doctor whistling as if he were calling a dog. 'Here ... Here, boy ...' he coaxed. The Wirrrn's eyes turned away from her and began moving towards the sounds. The Doctor fell silent, and the Wirrrn hesitated. Then it resumed its pursuit of Sarah. She switched off the torch, darted a few steps to the right in the pitch darkness, then crouched quite still, holding her breath. Again the Wirrrn stopped. Its eyes began to glow a bright fierce orange. The menacing rattle sounded. Sarah found herself mesmerised as the Wirrrn's eyes swung hypnotically before her. She could feel it tantalising her. Then her blood ran cold as she heard what sounded like sharp intakes of breath which rapidly grew into a rhythmic roaring, like the sound of a gigantic bellows. The creature was sniffing her out ...

The Doctor whistled again, this time from her right. The Wirrrn hovered uncertainly a moment, then moved swiftly towards the invisible figure.

'Torch, Sarah. *Torch*,' screamed the Doctor. Sarah switched on the torch and waved it recklessly about. The Wirrrn swooped towards her. She crept backwards, step by step, shining the torch-beam directly into the creature's eyes. With a rattle of triumph the Wirrrn reared up over her. She froze as something crumpled against the backs of her legs. She dropped the torch and toppled backwards into the disintegrated corpse of the Wirrrn Queen ... At the same instant she heard the Doctor shouting into the communicator. 'Now, Rogin. *Now*.'

A blinding blue-white flash lit up the Cryogenic Chamber. Sarah glimpsed the huge pincer slicing down at her. There was an ear-splitting shriek, and the sound of a massive body thrashing about in agony. Something soft and rubbery brushed across Sarah's face. A sickly burning smell filled the darkness. She lay among the rotting tentacles of the Wirrrn Queen shivering with nausea and choking from the acrid fumes. Then came the sound of the crippled Wirrrn crawling slowly away from her, and moaning with a croaking, gurgling cry which reverberated around the chamber until it died away into silence. As it gradually faded, the comforting gentle humming of the Cryogenic Systems resumed and the familiar faint glowing reappeared in the pallets. All around her the Chamber came back to life. Sarah closed her eyes in relief but before she could haul herself to her feet, she suddenly felt extremely dizzy. She keeled over on her side in a dead faint just as the Doctor reached her ...

8

A New Beginning

In the Flight Control Module of the Transporter
Vessel, the tension was becoming unbearable. Harry,
Rogin and Vira waited anxiously for news from the
Cryogenic Chamber. Sarah's piercing cries and the
bizarre shrieks of the Wirrrn still rang vividly in
their ears. Harry was hunched over the communicator set calling again and again. 'Doctor ... Sarah
... are you all right? Come in please ... Doctor, can
you hear me ...?' But there was no reply, only a
relentless silence. Vira kept watch on the Launch
Area through the video scanner, while Rogin, grim-
faced, monitored the Transporter's generator systems.

'We cannot maintain this level of power indefi-
nitely, Commander,' he warned.

As if in reply, the Doctor's voice suddenly came
through on the communicator. 'Rogin, whatever
happens don't let the power fade. We've won the first
round ... and I've managed to feed some energy into
the Cryogenic Systems, but there's very little to
spare ...'

'You have done well, Doctor,' interposed Vira.

'Thank you,' came the Doctor's reply. 'But if the
Wirrrn should detect our power source, you could be
in grave danger. You had better electrify the Launch
Dock.'

Rogin interrupted to explain that such a plan was impossible since the Transporter Vessel was moored to the Satellite by Synestic Locks.

'How very inconvenient, Rogin,' came the Doctor's disappointed voice. 'I should have realised: if you energise the Docking Area you may reverse the Synestic Fields and push the Transporter Ship out into Space.'

'Exactly, Doctor,' murmured Rogin.

There was a short silence. The Doctor spoke slowly and pointedly over the intercom. 'Well, you ought to think of something, Rogin, before the Wirrrn think of you ...' The communicator went dead again. Harry tried to re-establish contact, but without success.

Rogin turned to Vira, his face filled with dismay. 'Commander, I shall soon be forced to reduce power ... our generators will be needed for the transfer to Earth ... we cannot risk a malfunction.' Vira nodded gravely.

Harry sensed a certain irresolution in the manner of his two companions. 'Don't forget,' he warned. 'If the Wirrrn should get into the Cryogenic Chamber there won't be any transfer to Earth.'

In the Cryogenic Chamber, Sarah sat propped against the elevator shaft, recovering from her ordeal. She had regained consciousness to find herself wrapped in the Doctor's voluminous jacket, and the Doctor bending anxiously over her. She was still shivering with cold, and beginning to notice the effect of the oxygen system being shut down. She kept a wary eye on the opening into the Access Chamber, just visible in the restored glow of the pallets, while the Doctor bustled about the chamber checking his circuits leading from the junction box. One set was feeding power into the pallet Revivification Systems, while the other supplied the improvised 'electric fence' around the lower section of the chamber walls, and also the trailing cable with which the Doctor had fought off the Wirrrn attacker.

'Not bad for a lash-up, eh?' he grinned. 'But I hope the insulation will stand it,' he added, gesturing round at the pallets on floor level which were still occupied by dormant humans.

Sarah nodded towards the Access Chamber. 'The Wirrrn know where we are now,' she whispered, clutching the Doctor's jacket closer to herself for warmth.

The Doctor waved the torch about under his chin. 'You pulled such faces,' he chuckled in an effort to reassure Sarah. 'I don't think the Wirrrn will be in a hurry to come back ...'

Without warning the Access Chamber was flooded with light. Sarah shielded her eyes against the intense glare which temporarily obliterated her view of the entrance. 'Why have they turned the power back on?' she cried. The Doctor shrugged. Still carrying the free-running cable, he advanced towards the Access Chamber, motioning Sarah to stay where she was. Just as he reached the entrance, a distorted gabbling suddenly burst out all around them. For a second Sarah imagined that the sleeping humans in the

Cryogenic Chamber had suddenly revived, and that they were shouting in unison at her in a language she did not understand. She rushed to the Doctor's side in terror.

They stood in the Access Chamber listening to the eerie cacophony echoing around them. It was punctuated by harsh squeaks and hoarse whistlings. Gradually, there emerged a ghostly whisper, the shadow of Noah's human voice. 'Vira ... Vira ... hear me ...'

The Doctor indicated to Sarah to keep quiet, and went over to the intercom panel set into one of the Access Chamber systems consoles. He flicked the talkback button. 'What do you want, Noah?' he called.

A hostile buzzing issued from the intercom. Through it rose Noah's hollow whispering. 'Your resistance is useless. We control the Satellite.' The vicious buzzing increased as if in approval of Noah's words.

'And we control the Cryogenic Section,' said the Doctor defiantly. 'I repeat, what do you want?'

'Go now ... your lives will be spared,' came Noah's blurred reply.

'Impossible,' shouted the Doctor contemptuously.

The babble of Wirrrn voices reached a crescendo of furious anger. Noah's words struggled to be heard. 'Let ... Vira ... speak ... She is Commander ...'

The Doctor waited a moment, then he said, 'Vira is occupied with the revivification of her people.'

The buzzing of the Wirrrn reached a deafening roar. Again Noah's voice rose above it, this time filled with scorn for the Doctor's attempted bluff. 'That cannot be; the systems are isolated.'

The Doctor gave an exaggerated laugh. 'You forget, Noah, I have quite a way with electronics.'

'You lie,' Noah screamed, his voice breaking into monstrous gasps and screeching sounds. 'I am the Swarm Leader ... I guarantee your safety ... if you leave the Sleepers for us.' The Doctor said nothing. The Wirrrn gradually fell silent, then Noah hissed, 'If you refuse ... we will suffocate you.'

Sarah stared at the Doctor with frightened eyes. She remembered only too well the terrible sensation of breathlessness when the TARDIS had first materialised in the Satellite's Control Centre, and also during her ordeal inside the conduits. The Doctor gazed at the intercom panel, his face filled not with anger or hate, but with a kind of infinite weariness. He closed his eyes, racking his brains for some stratagem with which to defeat the Wirrrn. After a long pause, during which the angry murmurs from the Solar Chamber began to rise again, he started to speak very quietly, in a last appeal to Noah.

'Noah ... please listen to me ... if there remains within you any trace of your humanity—if you have any memory of the human you once were ... leave the Terra Nova ... lead your swarm into Space—that is where the Wirrrn belong ... not on Earth ... Earth is for the humans ... Do you remember the Earth, Noah? ... the wind ... the sea ... the sky ... dawn and sunset ...'

Noah broke in with a prolonged sighing voice which sounded through the chambers long after the intercom went dead. 'I... have ... no memory of ... the Earth ...'

In the Transporter Control Module, Harry had begun to fear the worst. There had been no contact with the Doctor since his warning about a Wirrrn attack on the Docking Sector, and he was also anxious for news of Sarah after her heroic success in reaching the Cryogenic Chamber. He was staring gloomily at the video scanner, wishing there were some simple way of returning to his office at UNIT Headquarters and forgetting all about Satellites and giant locusts and travelling Police Boxes.

Suddenly he leaned forward to look more closely at the fluorescent screen. 'I say, Rogin,' he murmured. 'I don't want to be an alarmist, but there's something moving out there.'

Rogin swung round and adjusted the scanner. A blurred, moving shape came into focus; three Wirrrn were crawling across the Docking Area towards the struts leading up to the Transporter's open maintenance hatch. At once Rogin manoeuvred himself over to the Propulsion Unit Panel. He began to operate a series of keys, muttering mechanically to himself. 'Particle Emission Phase: initiated ...' A colourful illuminated scale began to register on the panel. 'Acceleration to Tachyon Phase ... Negative Thrust ... Go.' The Transporter was enveloped in a piercing whine. It vibrated and shuddered at its anchorage. 'The Synestic Locking Field is holding,' Rogin called above the din.

All at once, the view of the Docking Area on the scanner was obliterated by a brilliant blue glare. After a few seconds, Rogin shut down the Propulsion Unit. The incandescent glare faded gradually away, revealing in the centre of the Docking Section a shapeless blob of colourless matter like melted glass. It was the fused remains of the three Wirrrn.

'Good show, Rogin,' cried Harry. 'That singed their whiskers!'

Vira sat staring blankly at the massive crystal shimmering beneath the Transporter. 'I wonder if Noah ...' she began, then she lapsed into silence.

'Commander?' Rogin inquired gently.

Vira immediately recovered herself. 'It is of no importance,' she said firmly.

'Are you all right over there?' The Doctor's voice boomed over the communicator.

'Doctor!' said Harry. 'Yes, we're fine, thanks. Nice to hear from you at last.' Harry quickly explained what had happened.

'They're up to something clever,' the Doctor muttered grimly. '... For some reason they've restored the power here ...'

A series of warning lights flickered in front of Rogin. He leaned over and adjusted the scanner so that it showed the outside of the Transporter hull, and the great silver shape of the Terra Nova turning slowly against the multitude of stars ...

Floating eerily from around the outside of the Solar Chamber there came a cluster of Wirrrn. As they drifted into view, they linked their tentacles together, forming a chain which snaked its way slowly across towards the Transport Vessel. The Wirrrn looked like giant sea creatures, feeling their way through the deep.

Harry spoke rapidly into the communicator. 'Doctor, the Wirrrn have broken out of the Solar Chamber. They are approaching us. It looks as if the whole swarm is going to attack.'

Rogin glanced across at Vira. 'Commander, if the Wirrrn break into the hull we shall be lost. The internal bulkheads have a low stress tolerance ...'

On the scanner, the Wirrrn leader could be seen feeling with its antennae for a suitable gripping point on the hull of the Transporter Vessel.

'Have you all gone to sleep?' shouted the Doctor. 'Rogin, cut the power. We're coming out.' Rogin obeyed. They heard the Doctor conferring with Sarah, then he added, 'Rogin, if the Transporter has an Automatic Flight System then initiate it at once, and evacuate the ship.'

Vira turned to Rogin in shocked protest. 'I forbid this. If we sacrifice the Transport Vessel we have no hope of returning to Earth ...'

Rogin said nothing, but pointed to the scanner screen. The Wirrrn leader had now secured itself to the Transporter hull; one by one the creatures clambered over the 'bridge' formed by the others. The Wirrrn were soon swarming all over the hull. A sickening tearing sound rang through the Ship; warning lights flickered on the panel in front of Rogin. 'The Wirrrn have pierced the hull in the Stabiliser Unit, Commander,' he cried. 'The sealing shutters are operating.'

Rogin frantically began to programme the Transporter for Automatic Launch in accordance with the Doctor's instructions. He did not understand the Doctor's intention, but he had come to trust and respect the shambling, eccentric stranger.

Harry manipulated the scanner, panning down towards the Transporter Propulsion Unit. What he saw sent shivers along his spine—a huge Wirrrn was tearing through the hull with its pincer as easily as a plough cutting a furrow in the soil. It was rapidly ripping a hole large enough for itself to enter. The whine of the Ship's generators, the shrill scrambling of the Wirrrn and the shriek of tearing metal combined into a deafening cacophony. More warnings suddenly appeared on the panels as the internal bulkheads began to yield.

'The Wirrrn have entered the Transport Vessel,' Rogin shouted, pushing Harry towards the hatch in the floor of the Control Module. 'You have four minutes to leave the Ship and clear the Launch Area before the Dock Shield opens and the Dock depressurizes to vacuum.' Harry nodded and followed Vira down the alloy ladder. All around them, the Transporter resounded with the Wirrrn's onslaught as they clambered hastily down the servicing tunnels, desperately making for the maintenance hatch before the Wirrrn could penetrate into the bowels of the Vessel. At any moment, a giant pincer might slice through a bulkhead, or a panel might open to reveal a rearing Wirrrn, its claw poised in triumph, barring their escape.

They reached the maintenance hatch safely and

Rogin caught up with them as they slid down the struts to the Launch Deck. At the same moment, the Doctor and Sarah emerged from the airlock and they all met beneath the gigantic propulsion nozzles, where the twisted remains of the three Wirrrn lay like a vast glass sculpture. The Doctor gestured to Harry to escort Sarah and Vira back through the airlocks into the main Satellite. Harry tried to object to deserting the Doctor and Rogin at such a vital moment, but the Doctor pushed him firmly away. Soon Harry and the two women were making their way cautiously towards the Control Centre where the TARDIS stood patiently waiting. To their amazement and relief they did not encounter any Wirrrn as they crept through the chambers and tunnels of the Satellite.

With the Transporter's motors thundering above their heads as the Tachyon Drive prepared to 'go critical', Rogin and the Doctor each ran to one of the main anchorage struts beneath the propulsion nozzles. Rogin pointed to the chronometer bracelet on his wrist, and then held up two fingers. The Doctor nodded and brandished the sonic screwdriver; Rogin nodded and held up his synestic key. They both immediately set to work to release the Synestic locks—three in number—on the main struts. Having completed the first one, Rogin glanced at his wrist. The chronometer scale showed barely a minute remaining before the huge circular shield, a hundred metres above them, opened like the 'iris' in a camera, allowing the atmosphere inside the Launch Area to evacuate into Space.

The Doctor had also completed the release of his synestic anchorage. They both made for the third and final lock, and arrived at the strut together. The Doctor motioned Rogin to take refuge in the safety of the airlocks. Rogin shook his head and bent down to deal with the remaining magnetic clamp. 'Get into the airlock, man,' the Doctor screamed in Rogin's ear. '... There's no sense in us both being disintegrated.' He tried to pull Rogin away from the strut. With a sudden lightning movement, Rogin stood up, catching the Doctor neatly on the chin with his head. The Doctor slumped heavily on to the deck.

Rogin dragged him across to the airlock and dumped him inside. He closed the outer shutter and ran back to the third synestic lock. On his chronometer bracelet the red arc showed just five seconds to zero. As Rogin released the last clamp, he was enveloped in a deathly chill: the air was sucked out of his lungs, and the blood began to boil in his veins as the Docking Section de-pressurized. Far above him, the elegant 'iris' shield was opening to allow the Transporter to launch itself into Space. He crumpled with a soundless scream ...

A few moments later, the Launch Area was filled with a searing plasma discharge. Rogin's body was transformed into a shapeless and colourless crystal in microseconds. Almost imperceptibly at first, the huge Transport Vessel separated from the Launch Assembly and began to climb away from the Docking Area. The very gradual acceleration was designed to disturb the Satellite's orbit as little as possible.

* * *

In the Control Centre, Sarah, Harry and Vira—watching on the main scanner—felt the slightest jolt. They stared in silence as the Transport Ship moved slowly away from the Terra Nova. Of the swarming Wirrrn there was no trace. The massive, ovoid craft began to accelerate into the depths of Space, its Tachyon Propulsion System leaving a brilliant blue aura in its wake. It grew smaller and smaller, finally becoming indistinguishable among the myriad stars. The luminous 'comet' tail lingered a little longer, then it too faded into nothing.

At last, Vira spoke. 'The Doctor and Technop Rogin must have perished instantly.' Sarah turned away from the scanner, stifling the sobs that rose in her throat. Harry moved over to her side, and put his arm gently round her shoulders.

'Come on now, old girl,' he said. 'You know he'd have wanted you to be brave.'

Sarah shook her head. 'It's such a waste,' she murmured.

'Not if it means that Vira's people are saved,' said Harry consolingly. 'I think we've seen the last of the Wirrrn.'

But Sarah was overwhelmed; she looked up at Harry, her eyes brimming with tears. 'Harry, I just can't believe it ... I just can't.'

'What can't you believe, Sarah?' boomed a familiar voice. The Doctor was standing in the entrance to the neighbouring Control Chamber, massaging his bruised chin. They were all too stunned to move or speak. The Doctor walked sadly across to Vira. He took her gently by the arm. 'Rogin is dead,' he said.

'He sacrificed himself so that the Satellite would be saved.' Vira nodded and turned slowly away towards the Cryogenic Systems Monitor Panel.

Sarah at last found her voice. 'Doctor ... how did *you* escape ... ?'

'Thanks to Rogin's bravery—and perhaps also to something else ...' The Doctor's words tailed off as he turned to stare at the scanner screen where the Transporter had disappeared among the stars.

'Something else, Doctor?' asked Harry, puzzled.

The Doctor walked over to the scanner. 'Yes, Harry. Some vestige of the indomitable human spirit, perhaps.' He turned to face them. 'Was Noah one move ahead of us all the time ... and even of the Wirrrn at the end ... ?'

Vira looked at the Doctor in astonishment. 'You mean that Noah deliberately led the Swarm into the Transporter?'

The Doctor smiled and nodded. 'I took a gamble that he would, and that ...'

The Doctor was interrupted by a rapid bleeping; an indicator pulsed on the External Communications Panel. Vira stared at it for a moment, then hurried over and touched a switch. 'Project Terra Nova ... The Commander,' she said crisply, identifying herself. Above the faint mush of static they gradually distinguished the distant murmur of the Wirrrn Swarm. A single, clearly human voice emerged and softly filled the Control Chamber.

'Farewell ... Farewell, Vira ...'

Vira stretched her arms out towards the scanner. She struggled to speak, but could not. Her arms fell back to her sides, and she stood motionless. All at once, one of the billions of tiny points of light flickering on the screen flared up like a supernova. For a moment it blazed, then it disappeared into nothingness.

'The Transport Ship's exploded,' Harry gasped. The Doctor walked thoughtfully away a few paces and then looked back at the scanner.

'Infinite Mass,' he muttered to himself. 'Noah had absorbed all Dune's technical knowledge. He must have known that would happen. He deliberately neglected to activate the plasma stabilisers.'

Sarah looked at the Doctor in amazement. 'You mean Noah sacrificed the Wirrrn for our sakes?' she cried.

Vira spoke with firm emphasis. 'Noah sacrificed *himself* for the sake of his people here,' she said.

The Doctor nodded and smiled at her. 'Now you can at last begin the great awakening of your people,' he said. But Vira shook her head. She was contemplating the Cryogenic Systems Monitor Panel which indicated that the initiation of the Main Revivification Phase was imminent.

'It is too late,' she murmured. 'Without the Transport Ship we have no means of reaching Earth.' The Doctor frowned. He glanced irritably at Sarah and Harry, as if this latest difficulty were their fault. Vira moved towards the panel, her hand raised, as if she were about to cancel the Revivification Process once and for all, and abandon the great plan which had succeeded thus far against incalculable odds.

The Doctor rushed forward and seized Vira's arm.

'Wait,' he cried. 'The Terra Nova Project will still be fulfilled. You can use the Matter Transmitter to reach Earth.'

Again Vira shook her head. 'There is no receiver on Earth. It is an internal system only.'

The Doctor put his hands on Vira's shoulders and looked earnestly into her eyes. 'If you and your people will trust me,' he said, 'I can go down to Earth and fix something up for you. With a little bit of juggling at this end we should be able to make it all work.' Vira stared at the Doctor as if he were demented. 'Oh, I realise that you'll have to travel one at a time,' he shrugged. 'And of course it will require enormous power; but I am sure that your Solar Power engineers will be able to oblige,' he added with a smile.

Vira opened her mouth to object, but the Doctor broke in briskly, with a gesture towards the Cryogenic Systems Panel. 'Look,' he cried. 'It's almost "reveille". We must make a start.'

Everyone followed the Doctor as he strode into the adjacent Control Chamber. Vira stared open-mouthed as the Doctor unlocked the door of the TARDIS. 'Old faithful,' he murmured affectionately, patting the chipped and faded blue paintwork.

Vira gasped in disbelief. 'Do you ask me to accept that you are intending to convey yourself to Earth ... by means of this ... this obsolete artefact?'

The Doctor looked grieved. He rubbed his finger across the dirty frosted-glass panes in the door, and grimaced at the blackened skin. 'This,' he said proudly, 'is a vintage specimen of Time And Relative Dimensions In Space technology—TARDIS—and, far from being obsolete, it has not even been invented yet.'

The Doctor adjusted his charred hat to a jaunty angle, and turned to step into the TARDIS. He collided with Harry who, hands firmly thrust into his pockets to avoid the temptation to tamper with anything, was about to enter with Sarah.

'Where do you two think you are going?' he demanded.

'Oh, you're bound to need a helping hand down there, Doctor,' Sarah laughed. 'You always do . . .'

Harry smiled apologetically. 'The Brigadier did ask me to keep an eye on you, Doctor,' he said.

The Doctor frowned, then he motioned them inside. 'Very well, just this once,' he agreed grudgingly. 'But you'd better both put some warm things on— one never knows what the weather's going to be like.' Sarah and Harry disappeared eagerly inside.

The Doctor turned to Vira. 'We shouldn't be very long,' he said.

'I shall expect you . . . soon,' replied Vira. 'Meanwhile I must return to the Cryogenic Chamber. The Main Phase is beginning.'

Sarah and Harry reappeared in the doorway of the TARDIS, clad in waterproofs and wellington boots.

'Back soon,' cried the Doctor, waving the jelly-baby bag. He broke off a piece from the melted contents and threw the bag to Vira. 'Good luck,' he called.

Vira caught the bag neatly. 'Good . . . luck . . . ?' she repeated the unfamiliar phrase to herself, puzzled.

An extraordinary groaning sound made her look up. A bright yellow light was flashing on top of the strange blue box into which the Doctor and his companions had entered ... As she watched, the box faded and gradually disappeared.

Suddenly Vira smiled in recognition. 'Yes ... yes,' she cried. 'Good luck ...'

She tentatively broke off a small piece from the sticky lump in the bag and put it into her mouth. She grimaced, then she smiled and nodded in approval at the taste. She looked at the empty space where the TARDIS had stood. 'Good luck, Doctor ... and thank you,' she murmured.

She turned and left. In the Cryogenic Chamber, her people were awakening in their hundreds. At last her task had begun ...

TARGET STORY BOOKS

Fantasy And General Fiction

101537	Elisabeth Beresford AWKWARD MAGIC	(illus)	60p
10479X	SEA-GREEN MAGIC	(illus)	60p
101618	TRAVELLING MAGIC	(illus)	60p
119142	Eileen Dunlop ROBINSHEUGH	(illus)	60p
112288	Maria Gripe THE GLASSBLOWER'S CHILDREN	(illus)	45p
117891	Joyce Nicholson FREEDOM FOR PRISCILLA		70p
106989	Hilary Seton THE HUMBLES	(illus)	50p
109112	THE NOEL STREATFEILD CHRISTMAS HOLIDAY BOOK	(illus)	60p
109031	THE NOEL STREATFEILD EASTER HOLIDAY BOOK	(illus)	60p
105249	THE NOEL STREATFEILD SUMMER HOLIDAY BOOK	(illus)	50p

Humour

107519	Eleanor Estes THE WITCH FAMILY	(illus)	50p
11762X	Felice Holman THE WITCH ON THE CORNER	(illus)	50p
105672	Spike Milligan BADJELLY THE WITCH	(illus)	60p
109546	DIP THE PUPPY	(illus)	60p
107438	Christine Nostlinger THE CUCUMBER KING	(illus)	45p
119223	Mary Rogers A BILLION FOR BORIS		60p

0426 Film And TV Tie-ins

200187	Kathleen N. Daly RAGGEDY ANN AND ANDY (Colour illus)		75p *
11826X	John Ryder Hall SINBAD AND THE EYE OF THE TIGER		70p* ♦
11535X	John Lucarotti OPERATION PATCH		45p
119495	Pat Sandys THE PAPER LADS		60p ♦
115511	Alison Thomas BENJI		40p

†For sale in Britain and Ireland only.
*Not for sale in Canada.
♦ Film & T.V. tie-ins.

TARGET STORY BOOKS

'Doctor Who'

TARGET STORY BOOKS

'Doctor Who'

200020	DOCTOR WHO DISCOVERS PREHISTORIC ANIMALS	(NF)	(illus)	75p
200039	DOCTOR WHO DISCOVERS SPACE TRAVEL	(NF)	(illus)	75p
200047	DOCTOR WHO DISCOVERS STRANGE AND MYSTERIOUS CREATURES	(NF)	(illus)	75p
20008X	DOCTOR WHO DISCOVERS THE STORY OF EARLY MAN	(NF)	(illus)	75p
200136	DOCTOR WHO DISCOVERS THE CONQUERORS	(NF)	(illus)	75p

Ian Marter
116313 **DOCTOR WHO AND THE ARK IN SPACE** 50p

Terrance Dicks
116747 **DOCTOR WHO AND THE BRAIN OF MORBIUS** 50p*

Terrance Dicks
110250 **DOCTOR WHO AND THE CARNIVAL OF MONSTERS** 50p

Malcolm Hulke
11471X **DOCTOR WHO AND THE CAVE MONSTERS** 60p

Terrance Dicks
117034 **DOCTOR WHO AND THE CLAWS OF AXOS** 50p*

David Whitaker
113160 **DOCTOR WHO AND THE CRUSADERS** (illus) 60p

Brian Hayles
114981 **DOCTOR WHO AND THE CURSE OF PELADON** 60p

Gerry Davis
114639 **DOCTOR WHO AND THE CYBERMEN** 60p

Barry Letts
113322 **DOCTOR WHO AND THE DAEMONS** (illus) 40p

David Whitaker
101103 **DOCTOR WHO AND THE DALEKS** 60p

Terrance Dicks
11244X **DOCTOR WHO AND THE DALEK INVASION OF EARTH** 60p

Terrance Dicks
119657 **DOCTOR WHO AND THE DEADLY ASSASSIN** 60p

Terrance Dicks
200063 **DOCTOR WHO AND THE FACE OF EVIL** 60p

Terrance Dicks
112601 **DOCTOR WHO AND THE GENESIS OF THE DALEKS** 60p

† For sale in Britain and Ireland only.
* Not for sale in Canada.
♦ Film & T.V. tie-ins.

Wyndham Books are obtainable from many booksellers and newsagents. If you have any difficulty please send purchase price plus postage on the scale below to:

Wyndham Cash Sales
P.O. Box 11
Falmouth
Cornwall

While every effort is made to keep prices low, it is sometimes necessary to increase prices at short notice. Wyndham Books reserve the right to show new retail prices on covers which may differ from those advertised in the text or elsewhere.

Postage and Packing Rate

UK: 22p for the first book, plus 10p per copy for each additional book ordered to a maximum charge of 82p. **BFPO and Eire:** 22p for the first book, plus 10p per copy for the next 6 books and thereafter 4p per book. **Overseas:** 30p for the first book and 10p per copy for each additional book.

These charges are subject to Post Office charge fluctuations.